Howls of the Windy city

Book Four in the Lawrence Miller Ghost Stories Series

Garrick Blake

Contents

Chapter 1

It was just after sundown when I banged my forehead on another of the rusty pipes crisscrossing the narrow corridor. I'm not a tall guy, but the U-boat seemed to have been designed for a crew averaging about 5' 7", or for seamen that got more hunched and uncomfortable the longer they had to remain aboard.

Metal groaned around me and the light from my flashlight seemed to just chase the shadows around me as I made my way towards the bridge. Or the conning tower. Or whatever the German word was for where the captain spent his working hours.

Some places more than others seem to collect ghosts, and a World War II U-boat captured off the coast of Africa in 1944 was prime real estate for the paranormal set.

This particular boat had seemed cursed almost from the start, being damaged and returning to port all but three of its handful of patrols, spending more time in dry dock than the Atlantic.

I had the opportunity by coincidence, several years earlier, to see where this specific U-boat had been constructed. They make Mercedes-Benz cars there now, but the locals will always tell you that the U-boats were from the same complex of factories and docks. It's not pride, really, it's just that the Germans don't shy away from their history, the good and the terrible.

It is a dedication to truth, to looking at the facts and speaking about them honestly however painful they might be.

The blunt acceptance of their history is itself a rejection of fascism, where the facts are dictated by the state and they have no duty to reality at all.

Tapping noises from the hull grew louder as I made my way towards the bow, the hatch I had entered through on the deck above long closed and silent behind me. It was as if the metal was contracting, chilled by the depths of the Atlantic pressing in around it.

Ghostly crewmen hustled around me, as oblivious to my presence there with them as they were to the decades of time that had passed since this submarine was captured. They were shadowy echoes of an activity a living human had found important, and most of them likely weren't connected to actual spirits or souls or whatever it is that makes people, people. It's the most common type of haunting, noticeable and probably unsettling but ultimately harmless.

Some of these echoes, most, probably, represented 58 men captured with the boat and held in secret at Fort Ruston in Ruston, Louisiana. They were kept separate from other prisoners of war and even the Red Cross was denied access to them before they were repatriated to Germany in 1947, having been declared dead and lost at sea by their homeland years earlier.

If the Germans had known one of their submarines had been captured, they might have changed their ways of operating or, worse, known that the Allies had gained access to Enigma, putting the Allied invasion of Normandy in jeopardy.

The ghost I was here to visit was the other kind of entity; a tortured spirit trapped on the wrong side of the veil. The kind that makes noises and moves objects and troubles the living, in this case, the night security guard for the

Museum of Science and Industry in Chicago, where the Museum Ship that is the former U-boat U-505 now rests.

The submarine spent years after the war being towed around and shown off as a trophy, almost every piece of the interior having been removed for analysis by the War Department.

Most of what was around me were replacement parts, assembled long after the war with parts from the original factories. The post-war Germans provided these free of charge, wanting U-505 to be as complete as possible as a testament to German engineering. The good with the terrible. So very German of them.

Though he probably hadn't started off particularly terrible himself, the ghost of the last Captain of the U-505 had become problematic of late, loud banging and disrupted exhibits increasing in frequency and intensity as the trapped spirit grew more and more frustrated at its inability to access an eternal rest.

I don't know what the afterlife for a Nazi U-boat Captain looks like, and that's none of my business. I was there, after hours in a closed museum, to send him there.

Even relatively benign hauntings can grow worse over time. You can keep a tiger in a small space for a while, but eventually it begins to resent that and, later, eats whatever idiot keeps them imprisoned there or even whoever just comes to look.

Spirits can work like that as well. The press of eternity piles onto them and whatever grip they had on the mortal world begins to become less and less substantial to them. Their behavior becomes more erratic as they inevitably lose all connection to who they were. Everything left behind is pain and rage and they only have one outlet for that.

Ghosts can't create things. They can't leave a positive mark on the world around them. That is the job of the living, and I wish more of us realized that.

The only mark a ghost can leave on the world is disruption. Their madness spawns chaos and their time to contribute to the community for the greater good is over. The longer it has been, the worse it gets.

But I specialize in the worse and the weird, and as I flung open the hatch to the recreated bridge of the U-505 and confronted the captain that had shot himself in the head in front of his crew at the beginning of his final battle, I realized how out of my depth I was.

Chapter 2

He hung from the periscope by one arm, swinging around the apparatus like a deranged monkey. The captain's cap was set at an angle, covered in fresh blood and sporting a hole on one side near the temple.

His arms and legs seemed obscenely long on a squat torso, his skin bizarrely looking waterlogged as though it was stretched across a drowned corpse even though he had died decidedly dry. Jagged nails and scraggly hair belied his military background, and his broken-toothed grin gleamed sickly in the sallow light of the re-constructed instrument panels.

Madness shone in his pus-colored eyes as they met mine and he became suddenly, starkly still, as though caught in a strobe light, his decades-long dance finally interrupted by a living visitor.

He shrieked, and the sound cut through me like razors and felt like it was intended to separate raw, bleeding flesh from bone.

I was already ducking to the left, reaching into my leather bag for some of the tools of the trade for a ghost hunter.

I also hoped this U-boat captain would miraculously understand English as I tried to de-escalate the situation.

"Ahoy, Captain!" I called, "You've got a shore excursion in the afterlife so I'm afraid you will be missing the buffet on the lido deck this evening."

The undead thing hopped off his perch and charged at me, his pace dictated by his weird physicality and that and only that kept him from reaching me in the first moments of the conflict. I knew if it came down to grappling, I was dead. His undead muscles were like steel cords under brine-bloated skin and mine are honed with infrequent spin classes under an exfoliated and well-moisturized casing.

My hand closed around a small brown paper sack in my messenger bag, and I flung it at the creature.

The bag burst against the thing's head, deploying its payload of salt all over it and briefly creating a cloud of it in the center of the room.

The ghost shook his head for a moment and then refocused his gaze on me, overall unaffected by enough salt to send even the most powerful normal ghost fleeing the scene and sometimes our reality entirely.

I wasted no time opting for the better part of valor, darting out the narrow hatch and back to the cold steel grating of the submarine's central passageway and running with clanging steps towards the aft of the vessel.

Most of the hatches on either side were closed but several were open and only roped off so that visitors could see the painstakingly reconstructed chambers on either side without any need to step into them.

I quickly made it back far enough to be crowded by the diesel engines, thankfully long silent. Many Nazi troops serving on these U-boats returned home with hearing loss from months at sea with these massive engines, if they were fortunate enough to return at all.

My shoulder clipped a bulkhead or a pipe or a wheel mounted to the wall to control something or other, but I didn't bother to investigate what it was in the dim yellow illumination of the submarine.

I bumped my electromagnetic field detector with my hand and it activated, instantly casting its own light into the dark space. Green, yellow, and bloody red indicating not just paranormal energy around me, but a lot of it. Active and powerful and potentially violent in a way that can end a ghost story before the teller even gets to the good part.

I ducked to the left – wait, starboard - leaving the narrow passage for an even narrower gap between two giant metal boxes which either stored enough dried food for 50 people to last three months or maybe just something that makes a submarine go. I'm not a submarine mechanic.

The ghost howled behind me, the sound echoing weirdly in the confined space. It was difficult to tell, but the sound seemed to be coming from closer and closer as I crawled through a small hatch and into the space just inside the hull of the U-boat.

I moved farther back, crawling over beams and wedging myself past the heavy steel plates of the ship, paint long etched into ornate patterns by the salt creep which was inevitable on vessels from the time period. In fact, I'm not sure it has improved much in the decades since the U-505 spent time underwater.

The sea isn't something humans have ever successfully kept out of places where it belongs or even just wants to go.

My hand brushed over satchels of herbs and sacred stones, and a brass bell sitting unused in my bag since all around me were the sounds of clanging metal already and our dear Captain was as unperturbed by the noise as he was by my bag of salt, of which I easily had another half dozen.

In fact, the weight of the suddenly useless salt seemed to lean heavily on me as I approached the bank of batteries which would have been charged by the sub's diesel engines.

I could hear the ghost of the captain rattling his way after me as I huddled in the very back of the boat. Wait. The aft.

I continued to dig through my bag looking for something, anything to stop this entity from keelhauling me when my fingers settled on the mostly full bottle of Gatorade.

I don't know what flavor it was, but it was blue if that helps. I had picked it up over a month earlier in an attempt to fight off a particularly vicious hangover, but a few sips had been more than enough motivation to just suffer through my well-earned pain.

Remember that experiment in middle school science class where positive and negative clamps were connected to graphite rods in a glass of water and salt was added which made oxygen bubbles form on the positive rod and hydrogen on the negative?

It doesn't matter, really, unless you're in an enclosed space like a German U-boat.

As the shattered skull of the captain peeked around the corner and committed to tearing me into scraps of meat in the aft of his command, I hit the batteries with a bag of salt and began to pour the Gatorade over the mess I had made.

A torpedo or well-placed depth charge would be terrible for a U-boat, but the real horror is in that middle school science experiment. Tiny bubbles of gas in a well-ventilated room are very different from those bubbles in an enclosed space. The water that makes up every ocean breaks up into hydrogen and oxygen, but the salt also breaks down into sodium and chloride, expressed as chlorine gas.

Seawater on the batteries of a submarine would short out the power, instantly casting the sub into pitch black darkness and then filling that same space with chlorine gas. Used as a weapon in World War One but outlawed for future conflicts because of the effect it had on people, especially their delicate lungs, it had nowhere else to go in metal cylinders fathoms underwater. You can argue with chemistry as much as you want, but there's a time limit.

An unpowered submarine in the dark with seawater fouled batteries with no way to surface or to even remain level would slowly sink to the bottom while filling with poison gas.

It didn't matter anyway. The batteries were fiberglass replicas, and my table salt and stale sports drink formulation was hardly some occult cheat code, but the effect was immediate.

The specter of the captain howled again and began to bounce off the steel walls around us, pantomiming a hysterical frenzy of bailing non-existent water and wiping down the equipment, decades having passed since he had enough brains in his skull to see the way things had changed around him, how the living can't be trusted to play fair.

I began to cough loudly and clutch at my throat, flailing around the room before collapsing to the deck.

"Abandon ship!" I gasped theatrically.

The U-boat fell silent as the captain apparently did just that, fading away as his spirit passed through the hull and into the dark museum. And presumably beyond that as well.

For a ghost bound to a location, getting them to leave that place is the simplest way to be rid of them. Once a spirit knows it can be somewhere else, it generally will choose to do so.

His destination was unimportant to me and always had been. I was here to sound the last call for a ghost that had overstayed his time in the realm of the living, and I was like the overworked bartender of the damned. And my evening was just getting started.

Chapter 3

I checked in with the night watchman another time before leaving the museum. I told him that the ghost would be gone, possibly forever, but that if there were additional issues, he knew how to reach me.

Rather than leave on the ground level, I exited the museum through a back storeroom in the basement. Past a long discontinued and packed away exhibit on communication technology, telegraph machines and Bakelite phones leading up to an old Nokia brick which would have been cutting edge the last time it was displayed for the public was a scratched and battered metal door so dented it was wedged into the frame.

It was a twenty-minute drive to my destination, but I wouldn't be driving. I had left my car in the garage at my hotel, and I had time to take the scenic route for fans of Chicago history.

Parts of the storied Chicago underground are still in use and heavily trafficked by various human authorities but other connected tunnels, winding their way under the oldest parts of the city are mostly abandoned. Long used by smugglers and a staple of prohibition Chicago, the underground today is a tourist destination, used for delivering freight and services around town while avoiding all the traffic topside.

Apart from the pedestrian tunnels linking several popular places above ground, utility tunnels, old speakeasy tunnels and abandoned subway tracks twist their ways under Chicago, a refuge for criminals and people who have just had enough of the rest of us and the other, darker, fouler things that inhabit this world without sunshine.

The pedway entrances are clearly marked above ground, but I wasn't using one of those.

This entrance under the museum linked with a ComEd utility tunnel, the conduit seeming to hum to itself in the darkness. I took a moment to test the half dozen flashlights I had stashed away in various pockets, changing out dead batteries and making sure I could get to each in an emergency.

I'd planned to make my way through the more popular tunnels to one or more of the performative restored speakeasies in the underground, nothing too dark or abandoned or restricted. Like any urban explorer, I intended to cling to plausible deniability if I should happen across any of the various authorities in the dark, be they police or night security guards or even just workers going about their business with the perfectly reasonable expectation of not bumping into some idiotic ghost hunter down in the dark.

Fully committing to the moment, I took a swig of room temperature whiskey from the oversized flask I had stashed in my inner jacket pocket. The booze-soaked history of Chicago deserved the respect I would give to a dear friend's wedding, at least. Open bars are only so open, after all. The contracted bartenders always try to wave you away when you ask for a drink and have left your pants back at the table with the weird aunt, no matter how much sense that made at the time.

I made it to the end of the ComEd tunnel with a ladder to the topside and found a boarded up opening into another tunnel which wasn't lit by friendly LEDs or tired halogen lamps.

A brick-lined space smelling of Lake Michigan and mugs of long dried beer and things best forgotten waited for me. Catnip for a history buff or for a ghost hunter and I was hopelessly both, so I set about pulling boards free just enough to squeeze through into the dark.

Skittering sounds preceded my journey into the enhanced night of the Chicago underground. Rats, probably, but my imagination provided countless alternative sources.

To say that this walk was Disneyland for a paranormal investigator still somehow sells it short. This paranormal nonsense deposits itself on locations like silt from the Mississippi or fertile loam from the Nile or generational trauma from any storied family.

It piles up, and it doesn't go away.

The corridor stretched out ahead of me, slowly curving right towards the lake, the concrete floor covered in dust and rodent droppings. Even the spiders knew there wasn't much point in spinning webs down here. The local bugs were used to navigating in the dark or they'd seek out richer places to hunt or scavenge.

I thumbed on a flashlight and crawled into the passageway, leaving the spare boards on the ground behind me. Worst case, someone would find them and put them back in the next week or so. I had no illusions that anyone would think to crawl in after me.

Overhead, the brilliant lights of the Chicago skyline bounced against the clouds and reflected from the questionable puddles on the streets and sidewalks, but down in the underground I was just someone alone in the dark. A smarter person would have been afraid. Anyone with an ounce of survival instinct would have just called a cab and ridden in conversation-free silence to his destination.

But that's not a very good story.

In addition to encouraging wayward spirits towards their eternal rewards in the afterlife, whatever that may look like, I am committed to gathering tavern-worthy tales of the process. Ghost stories bind us together as people. They teach us moral lessons and ease the transition all of us must someday take when crossing from the realm of the living into the lands of the dead.

They tell us, ultimately, what there is in the world around us that is worth being afraid of.

And as I shuffled through this long-abandoned corridor surrounded by pitch black darkness with only the LED-fueled spear of light before me, I could sense that a good story lay in front of me.

If I was fortunate enough to survive it to pass it along later.

Chapter 4

My ultimate destination was the penthouse-level restaurant on top of a twenty-something-story building built in the 1930's. The manager had contacted me about late night disturbances in the dining area. Shattered light bulbs and scattered flatware, broken plates and glasses and framed photos flung off the walls.

You know, standard stuff for a haunted place. And low stakes enough for me to take this casual stroll through the underground on the way.

From the photos I had been sent, the décor was exactly what you'd expect if the company had more respect for history than current trends in fine dining. Fireplaces and dark wood paneling dotted with framed art of fancy men hunting foxes and tall shelves of books no one had opened in decades. It was the kind of space where cold cucumber soup and finger sandwiches somehow count as food and make sense.

A simple haunting in a place where no one actually lives was exactly the balm my own spirit needed. Stakes so low I would need a backhoe to find them.

Ahead of me, somewhere out of the range of my flashlight, a stone clattered against the concrete floor. It sounded irregular, like a broken chunk of cement, and it was the last sound before the tunnel fell into a silence so absolute it hurt my head.

Previously, I had been able to hear the soft sounds of traffic overhead, the noise of vermin around me in the dark, the subtle signs of the life and death struggles of the rats and the insects, but all of that was gone as if it had never existed. An unreliable memory, it seemed.

But I followed the sound around the gradual bend in the corridor, just catching sight of a flowing floral skirt as it turned right towards the lake, following the bend in the tunnel.

One of the very real dangers of urban exploration is finding, by surprise, that some long-abandoned place isn't as abandoned as it is supposed to be. I mean ghosts and spirits and assorted haunts can be bad and all, but humans are the ultimate wild card in that scenario.

You can't know why a person would inhabit some dark, non-climate-controlled place with no running water and no paperwork at all granting them access and shielding them from liability, what kind of desperation would drive a person to be out there on the very edge of civilization without the safety net of a community and with no one knowing where they are or even if they are alive or dead.

It could almost only be someone bereft of reason or higher thinking, prone to spontaneous decisions and almost allergic to thinking things through or without any measurable self-preservation instinct.

Yeah, okay, I hear it.

Hustling to follow, and with no attempt at subtlety, I scuffed along the passageway. The feeble light from my hand only illuminated thin spears in the pitch darkness while my imagination filled in the details around me with silent cackling demons and the cavorting lost souls of the damned. My imagination is kind of an asshole, especially in the dark.

The air seemed heavier there, thick with the scent of damp stone and the whisper of old secrets waiting just beyond the reach of my flashlight. Every step forward felt like a negotiation with the unknown, but curiosity always managed to outweigh caution.

The light leaking through from the streets above was infrequent, but it lanced into the stygian darkness around me, illuminating irregular shapes on the stone floor and brilliantly illuminating dust and cobwebs in the air.

From time to time, I caught a glimpse of the figure moving ahead of me. While she didn't seem to be making any effort to ditch me there in the dark, she kept just far enough ahead that I only caught glances of sleeves or skirt, once seeing long red hair spill over a pale shoulder.

She made no sound in the darkness, never stumbling even though she carried no light of her own and mine barely reached her. There was no way it could illuminate her path for her.

I don't know how long I trailed along after her before I realized I was hopelessly turned around.

In my hometown Houston, Texas there is a system of tunnels that is miles long as well, linking most of the buildings downtown. During the summer months, the only safe way to walk around in the brutal heat is to avoid it, so I've spent a lot of time walking through those tunnels to grab lunch or pick up a quick gift or visit a convenience store, all without ever having to see the surface.

In the early days of my tunnel exploration, it was possible to get lost, but there are maps posted throughout and the time-honored activity of "prairie dogging" or popping one's head up above ground to ascertain location is pretty common, especially for new people just starting jobs downtown.

But I had no frame of reference for this set of tunnels. There were no handy maps posted in whatever area I was in, and I realized it had been quite a while since I had seen even a boarded-up stairwell or exit sign.

The section of the tunnel I was in was older, possibly closer to the lake, judging by the frequent slow drips of water through the brickwork. But I was more than a little disoriented and wouldn't put any money on where I might end up even if I could find an exit to the surface.

Not all of the passages are mapped out even today and the older sections were likely connected to buildings that have been remodeled or torn down as the city grew skyward overhead so even if I happened across a stairwell it was possible, likely even, that it would end in a cement slab overhead or just collapse under my weight, having had no support from above for many years.

I turned a corner under a dusty brick archway and realized I had caught up to the figure, or, more accurately, she had stopped and waited for me.

She slowly turned to face me as my flashlight decided it was a good time to stutter and die in my hand.

"Hey, Lair," Meghan said, "We need to talk."

Chapter 5

Meghan O'Leary had joined me on a ghost hunt in Austin, Texas and, regardless of the details or motivations around the event, she had died there. I wasn't okay with it, and I had no expectations that I ever would be. Some of my many failures burn more brightly than others.

The shade had addressed me by name, so this wasn't an echo, some mindless remnant of a human or some human's emotions. The entity had agency, and she not only knew my name, but she knew the nickname I had firmly refused to adopt. The nickname Meghan O'Leary herself had first given to me. Over nachos, if I was remembering correctly, so in as sacred a space as cuisine gets outside of brunch.

"Nice to see you again, Meghan," I offered lamely, "What brings you to Chicago?"

"I don't have a lot of time," she stepped back from me, as though she didn't know I'm instinctively not much of a hugger, "I come with a warning for you."

"Sure. Toss it on the pile," I shook my head, "I'm so sorry about what happened in room 318. You shouldn't have died."

"Shut up, Lair," she laughed in that way that illuminated dark spaces, "I know that it isn't in your skill set, but listen."

I couldn't have looked away if I had wanted to. She looked exactly like she had before a ghost had blasted a hole in her chest with a borrowed electrical outlet.

A flowing skirt over combat boots and under a chunky sweater, glasses perched on her nose beneath a halo of untamed flame-red hair. As vibrant and self-assured as she had been back when she had a pulse.

"You've broken a very old covenant," she continued, "Ten thousand years old, at least, but still enforced and still a very big problem for you."

"I drink a lot, Meghan," I started, "But I'm almost 90% sure I didn't sign anything ten thousand years ago."

"Humanity did, Lair," she snapped, "and you broke the rules so if they don't take it out on you, they will take it out on the rest of us."

"I guess 'they' are the fairies?" I asked.

She winced. "They go by a lot of names but that is one of their least favorite."

"Obviously I'm going to step on my own ass in this interaction, Meghan," I said, exasperated, "Why are you the messenger for the Fair Folk."

"Come on, Lair," she grinned, "Why do you think I, specifically, would be chosen to carry word to you of your failures?"

I felt the blood rush to my face and then immediately drain from it as I struggled to turn on another flashlight. I could see her well enough, but only her, and this was the third flashlight I had tried to activate in a pocket with no success.

"You sent death to a world that hadn't seen it in thousands of years," she stepped forward in the dark, "and you did it to save your own hide, like you do everything, you whiskey-soaked asshole."

"Meghan," I tried with my left hand to turn on another flashlight while I dug around in my bag with my right, "Austin ended way worse than I expected it to and I'm very sorry about that. And things have gone downhill consistently since then, so I'm pretty certain I'm not exactly steering this bus, but I cannot express how much I didn't want any of this."

"And is it always about what you want?" she yelled, suddenly rushing towards me.

I flung a handful of salt at Meghan's face, and she stopped her advance but shook her head and quickly stepped towards me again. Was it possible to get a bad batch of table salt? I thought that stuff had a fairly infinite shelf life. Or I've been wildly misled by Diners, Drive-ins and Dives.

As so many of us have, I suppose, in one way or another.

I staggered out the way I had come in, having no better plan and my sense of direction in emotional turmoil.

The dark corridors spiraled ahead of me in a confusing maze; blackness spotted with infrequent light from cracks and gaps at the base of the streets above – when streetlamps or headlights were in the right place at the right time. I couldn't see my footprints in the dust to retrace my steps, so I knew I was likely plunging deeper and deeper into the confusing cobweb of tunnels in the underground.

My thoughts were in no better shape. I had tried to process Meghan's death over and over and sometimes there just isn't enough whiskey in the world to make things make sense. I don't know if that says worse things about whiskey than it does about the world, but either way it isn't kind.

Meghan had sacrificed herself in room 318 with the idea that I could resolve the haunting afterwards. Or maybe that she could better resolve it from the liminal space between the living and the dead.

But either way, she hadn't consulted me first and I was still more than a little pissed about that. And sad.

And guilty.

The weight of responsibility ignores intent, and I had been crushed under it ever since.

I took a sudden, unplanned left and found myself on a walkway of wooden slats. I ran as fast as I could, seeing a brick opening on the other side.

And I almost made it before the rotted wood gave way under my unsubtle steps and I plunged into total darkness.

Chapter 6

Forever a part of Chicago's aviation history, in 1979 Flight 191 departed the gate and began the departing taxi for its trip to California. As it reached speed for take-off, one of the engines detached and rolled over the wing, destroying part of that as well.

The flight crew couldn't see the engine from the cockpit, so they thought the engine had simply failed. Protocol at the time, in the case of a failed engine at speed, was to ascend and then circle back to land for repairs.

In this instance, the wing failed and the plane flipped into a field. Loaded with enough fuel to get to LAX, the ensuing fireball resulted in the deaths of 271 passengers and crew in the deadliest aircraft disaster in America's history with the exception of September 11th.

In the weeks following, residents of the area would report people knocking on their doors, confused and asking where they were. Eventually, the strange visitors would wander off and disappear.

People still report a ghostly plane in the field or crowds of phantom people wandering around disoriented and aimless.

Some say that the echoes of that night still linger over the city, a silent reminder to those who pass through O'Hare or gaze up at departing planes. Tragedy can leave a kind of residue in places, a lingering sense of something unresolved. Sometimes, it feels as if the city itself breathes in these stories, holding them in its bones and bricks, whispering them back to anyone who listens closely enough.

Most airlines have since retired 191 as a flight number, as five Flight 191s have crashed resulting in 368 total deaths. As much as the airlines would like to forget, to move past these horrific events, Chicago remembers.

A little outside of town is a dilapidated bridge across a creek which has gathered legends around itself even as physical pieces have rotted away and passed into the running water below.

Locally known as Axeman's Bridge, the original story is still up for debate. In some tales, a reclusive former resident killed two trespassing children with an axe near the old bridge. In another, a man killed his whole family with an axe and then burned down his house, attacking the police when they showed up before being eventually gunned down while trying to flee across the bridge. After this much time, it hardly matters.

Visitors report late night clanging sounds, like the noise from an axe striking the steel girders of the old bridge or a ghostly house appearing through the trees that doesn't exist during the day.

Most terrifying, people have reported their cars stalling on the road to the bridge, with the surrounding woods falling silent before the sounds of screaming echo across the countryside.

Perhaps it's no surprise, then, that stories linger in places marked by tragedy, where the land seems to remember what happened upon it. Local lore suggests that the bridge and its surroundings carry an energy that unsettles even the most skeptical visitors. Shadows drift along the creek at night, and some claim to hear whispers on the wind, recounting fragments of the old stories or warning travelers to turn back. The bridge stands not just as a physical relic, but as a monument to the unresolved pain woven into Chicago's history.

Chapter 7

I woke up choking on dust in a tangle of decaying support timbers. This new area wasn't as dark as the area above, but only because at some point six flashlights had turned themselves on in my various pockets and I was lit up like I was selling mushroom gummies at one of the rare raves that didn't have a maximum age for participation.

I moved to start shutting them off one by one and noticed pretty quickly that my left shoulder was bruised if not dislocated and my left leg was maybe shorter than the right one now. At least the pain from it got to my brain more quickly and I assume that's how that works.

I'm not a doctor.

With the final flashlight I looked around the pit I had fallen into. There was a drain in the dirt floor and walls were lined with moldy, horizontal wooden slats.

I could see the remains of the walkway overhead, but there was no way the slat walls would support a climb up.

Finding a narrow crawlspace I could access behind some damp boards, I set about prying them free. Rusted nails and moldy wood weren't much of an obstacle, but I quickly regretted not bringing gloves.

The smell of rat droppings and ammonia filled my nostrils as I made my way forward on hands and knees, hoping blindly that this passageway might open up somewhere with an exit to the surface or any indication of where I was exactly.

I crawled out into a room made from fire-blackened brick built around a blue-patinaed copper tank with matching pipes snaking around it.

When prohibition was the law of the land, some local pubs turned to the mafia to acquire booze for their customers, fostering a speakeasy vibe throughout Chicago which still hasn't gone away.

Other pubs opted to brew their own alcohol underground, in setups just like this one. Often, the mob would object to this assuming the bar in question was buying booze from a competing family. Very few local brew operations survived the mafia purges to remain open under the same management after prohibition was officially declared a failure.

There was a sagging, wooden spiral staircase in a corner that disappeared into a patch on the ceiling that my flashlight couldn't quite light up.

I was just going through the thought exercise all urban explorers and haunted house enthusiasts eventually entertain: Should I take slow and careful steps across unknown flooring or madly dash across them so I can get to the other side before it decides to collapse, when movement in the back corner of the room caught my attention.

A potbellied man with a receding hairline and a stained apron shoveled invisible fuel into the fire box under the giant boiler, presumably wood or coal gone from the area for around a century.

He went about his work without looking my way, eventually touching the copper vessel with the back of his hand as though checking the temperature before walking briskly past me and up the rotting stairway, his steps sure and carrying the confidence of long routine.

He was an echo, a remnant of human activity left on this place like a cyst of paranormal activity, hurting nothing and oblivious to the passage of time around him. He would never see me, as he was trapped in a time before I existed and probably completely unaware that the copper vat had been out of use for decades.

His escape up the stairs didn't help me because he was weightless and would likely make the same exact trip with the same exact steps even after the stairs crumbled to dust.

Hopefully, the soul of the man had traveled to his eternal reward so I wouldn't need to be ushering anyone to the other side. Echoes are often sad but in addition to being disconnected to the changes around them and immune to the passage of time, they rarely have anything to do with a human soul, or whatever part of us it is that makes a ghost in the first place.

Bereft of options, I began to carefully ascend the decaying stairs myself with my flashlight held in my teeth so I could keep both hands on a railing. The creaks and pops of the ancient wood were unnerving, but I eventually arrived at a wooden trap door.

Pressing the door open slowly elicited a fresh round of ominous sounds from my rickety platform as an irregular section of camouflaged floorboards rose into the darkness above me.

I crawled up into the space above the covert brewery and rolled over onto my back before pressing the floor back into place.

I had disturbed decades of dust and could clearly see the outline of the trap door from this side, but regular traffic and occasional sweeping would have rendered it invisible.

The room I was in was a storeroom of some kind, with racks for barrels along two walls and narrow steps beside a concrete ramp that both led up to a battered wooden door.

It was locked, but the lock itself was so old that picking it with my twelve-dollar set of tools from Amazon was almost recreationally easy. I knew going into this subterranean hike that there were likely places that would be secured in some way to prevent casual access, so I was ready for those. In the event of Top-Secret government laboratory or the lair of some reclusive super villain, I had planned to just go around. My personal Justice League included a fairy contract witch in Austin, Texas and the remains of a werewolf pack a time zone to the left so any bat signal I could set off for help had bigger issues than just my being underground.

The door opened into a brick-lined room with a few alcoves containing the remains of rotted furniture and a long bar along one wall, warped in a way that indicated this place had been flooded long before and never accessed again afterwards.

I found a stack of paper "Yahoo" cards, apparently an early version of Bingo which was probably abandoned and renamed because of the second O needing a little number two beside it.

Maybe the space could pretend to be a harmless gaming hall and social club if the authorities raided it for serving alcohol? I don't know. I haven't had to hide alcohol consumption beyond enhanced coffee creamer at work, so I'm hardly an expert. An HR nightmare, for sure, but not an expert.

A rack which probably held glasses at one point swung open after a little prodding and I found myself in another small stairwell. Thankfully, this one was brick and seemed solid enough as I ascended towards the street again.

It ended in a small chamber that I blundered into before realizing I wasn't alone.

I shared the space with a slight woman in a clinging black dress, moss-green hair hanging around her head like a crown. Her flat-black eyes bored into my own.

"Hey, Morrigan," I waved lamely, "Fancy meeting you here."

Chapter 8

She looked at me without blinking for an uncomfortable amount of time, like a bird watching a delicious bug on a branch or a cat staring at the red dot from a laser pointer. Potentially murderous either way.

The Morrigan, who was currently in Chicago, is the Irish goddess of . . . She's the goddess of a lot of stuff, actually. And also, she's maybe not really a goddess by most definitions.

She didn't create the world or the people in it. Like all Irish deities she was just really good at not dying and never bothered to do it.

She's the aspect of War and Death, the Defender of Women and the Home and Hearth. She is an aspect of the

Sovereignty of Kings and, possibly most famously, she is the Chooser of the Slain. She determines who lives and who dies in any conflict, and she ushers the souls of the fallen into the afterlife.

But she's old, and that inevitably colors our interactions. I have to remind myself that she watched the Romans attempt to take the Irish island, and that she remembers cattle being the only currency and that the whiskey she first remembers was made illegal for hundreds of years by the British because it possibly caused blindness. As if that was a deterrent.

And also, she is kind of my employer, I guess, though I haven't figured out where to send the invoices. And I'm way too terrified to ask.

I sat down on the wood floor and opened a bottle of water, had a long drink and set it in front of me. I pulled out a flask of whiskey as well and poured two shots into matching steel cups.

My tactical vest was loaded with pockets, and I wasn't one to waste any of them.

The Morrigan folded herself into a seated position across from me, somehow without creasing her dress or exposing anything which would result in my death. A neat trick, honestly.

"That was a Púca," she announced, strangely. She drank her cup of whiskey somehow more smoothly than I had the water. Living for a long time seemed to involve drinking a lot.

"What?" I asked, mustering every bit of conversational skill I had developed over a lifetime of team meetings and status calls.

"A Púca," The Morrigan shook her head, "a shapeshifter, hired to pretend to be your friend Meghan to upset you and keep you off your toes."

"That's a dick move," I objected, "And why my salt bomb didn't work, obviously. Who would do that?"

"You've made an enemy of one of the Fae courts," she said, "and even if they aren't conventional in their means, Themselves can be expected to make every effort to collect on a debt."

"I annoy a lot of people," I admitted, "It's honestly my go-to move. But I haven't tried to start any shit with any fairy court."

"Your intentions don't matter at all to them," she took my flask and poured herself another generous drink, "You offended Themselves and they keep score."

"I suppose it's too late to tell you I don't believe in Púcas?" I asked, "Are you going to tell me that the Easter bunny and the tooth fairy are real, too?"

"Tooth fairies are very real," The Morrigan replied, "though they are poorly named. They collect the teeth of human children which are offered to them because it's easy, but in fact they prefer just about any bone from a living adult human."

"I hate everything you've just said," I took another drink from my flask, "and I'm going to not believe it anyway."

"Your beliefs," she shrugged, "like all beliefs, have no impact on your reality."

"How do I fix it with the Fae?" I asked, "How do I make it right?"

"I told you of your foolishness," she grinned mirthlessly, "and afterwards you sent them a monster that resulted in loss of life."

"The ghost Rougarou?" I wondered, "I just tried to send him away, not towards anyone."

"But he ended up killing several of them," she sighed, "and they are many centuries past being used to the death of their own."

"Whatever," I brushed that off as something I couldn't do anything about, "but that wasn't Meghan? She's not trapped here as a lost soul?"

"I took her to the Irish afterlife myself," The Morrigan said, "She died in battle, and she has earned her rest."

"So, she's okay?" I asked, "she's not suffering or trapped or anything?"

"She's got access to the Irish Ghost World, and all the ancient knowledge and beer and spirits brewed by the gods themselves."

"And she's not," I hesitated, "She's not mad at me?"

"She's too busy to be angry, child," The Morrigan looked almost like she pitied me for the question, "She made her choice, and that's a better end than most get."

"When it's my time," I asked, "will I go to the Jewish afterlife or the one with all the books and the booze?"

"Not knowing what's after is part of the pain mortals pay in exchange for getting to make their own choices, Lair," she answered sadly.

"Shit," I muttered, "Most of my choices aren't worth that."

"Oh," she chuckled, "They most certainly are not. I once told you that you didn't have the good sense the gods granted to goats and since then I've realized that I was terribly uncharitable to goats."

"That's fair," I admitted, "Hurtful, but fair."

"Everything worth doing can be hurtful, Lair," she smiled sadly, "and most things that aren't."

"I assume this isn't a social call?" I asked, tipping the flask back again and passing it back to her.

"Your soul is in peril," she didn't pull any punches, I guess.

"When is it not?" I asked.

"Not your life, Lair," she talked to me like I was simple, "Your soul."

"I don't really do a lot with it," I shrugged, "I just try to make sure it doesn't make me look puffy."

"Yer a fecking eejit," she lapsed into her brogue, "Blindly runnin' into mortal peril as though it doesn't apply to ye."

"How else does one blindly run?" I was honestly out of ideas about that.

She took a moment to compose herself, a deeply unsettling moment for anyone sharing proximity with the Chooser of the Slain, even if he had generously shared his finite supply of whiskey with her.

"Lost souls are ahead of ye," she prophesied, "And the one that made them lost."

"Here?" I asked, "In Chicago?"

"Aye," she nodded quickly, "A grim sort o' ghost who can knock the soul right out o' the living and consume it."

"That's not a thing," I scoffed, "Ghosts don't have any sway over the souls of the living. They can fling things and start fires and stomp around attics, but nothing holds sway over a human soul. That's the whole reason we bother having them."

"What's a dumber animal than a goat?" The Morrigan asked. "That's not the reason you have a soul at all, ye git."

"Maybe a turkey?" I shrugged again, "Don't they drown when they look up at the rain?"

"That's a myth," she grabbed my flask again and I didn't fault her for that. I never fault anyone for that, if I'm going to be honest.

"Look who's talking shit about being a myth," I finished off the flask after taking it back and tucked it into a pocket, freeing another to be in a more accessible location. This was far from my first rodeo.

"The ghost is a killer," The Morrigan spat, "Not a clean killer, he drugged his victims and trapped them nearby, tortured them, abused them, and the abuse of their souls was as important to him as the desecration of their bodies."

"A ghost is a ghost, right?" I asked.

"Aye," she admitted, "To an extent. But this soul spent his life torturing and entrapping others, and his whole purpose was in damaging their souls."

"If I spent my whole life trying to host the best Oscar party, would I carry that ability into my haunting?" I was just trying to establish the rules here.

"A nacho cheese fountain will never make up for the exclusion of special effects awards from the broadcast," she answered.

“Someone just secured her invitation for next year,” I nodded.

“You won’t survive until next year,” she barked, “You won’t survive this night if we don’t take steps to prepare you.”

“I have reservations at a steak house tomorrow night, so I’m listening,” I replied.

“Your soul is vulnerable,” she said, “but we can make it less so.”

“Obviously, I would like to see the guide, or any associated white papers about this process,” I started, “Maybe an informative YouTube video? But I guess I would appreciate whatever you can do to protect me from the next part of my journey.”

She handed me a small metal raven skull on a leather cord, possibly pewter or maybe just lead.

“A single touch from this murderous ghost would strike the spirit from you, feeding your energy to his own,” she gestured at the little amulet, “Wearing this will prevent that from happening, though he can still hurt you in other ways.”

“How does it work?” I asked, slipping the cord over my head.

“It makes your soul mine,” she grinned again, like a coyote wandering through some hipster uptown chicken coop, "And I'm the one that decides what happens to souls that belong to me."

"There's always a catch with you immortal types," I answered.

But I didn't take the pendant off.

It made sense that The Morrigan was in Chicago. When you are responsible for making sure death and the afterlife is in good working order, you could be needed anywhere. But Chicago is also one of the most Irish places in the New World. From its earliest days as a settlement for Europeans on their way west, or even just on their way away from east, the Irish have congregated here.

Small communities of Irish Catholics grew and expanded towards the south side of the city, insular by necessity as they were excluded from most of the economic progress of the city even as they provided the labor for building it.

By the mid-20th century, the Irish had largely assimilated into American society. Some abandoned their faith as many do during a diaspora but a lot maintained it as another connection to home, a comfort. Faith is difficult to discount or quantify.

But American Irish Catholics are still Irish by The Morrigan's math. And there has been enough death in Chicago to attract her attention even without them all being Irish deaths.

Yet, for all their ties to the old ways and the city's relentless churn, there remained a quiet reverence in certain neighborhoods, marked by weathered shrines tucked between bars and corner stores. Echoes of ancient rituals mingled with the rhythm of L trains and sirens, creating a peculiar harmony unique to Chicago. Death here felt less like an ending and more like another chapter in the city's ongoing story. A transition observed but not feared, so of course there would be deities like The Morrigan quietly keeping watch.

We can find solace in the inevitable even if it is unpleasant to think about. And even if it drinks a lot of your whiskey and says terrifying things to you.

Chapter 9

She assured me again that Meghan was fine. Or as fine as it gets for dead people, anyway.

The Morrigan is not the aspect of being comforting, however, so eventually she walked back down the staircase I had just sweated my way up without any sort of farewell or any wishing of good luck.

I choose to believe it was implied.

Either way, I didn't get the impression she wanted me to follow her, and I still didn't trust that rotting stairwell. Also, I had already been that way, so it was crossed off my urban exploration list. I still had a long way to go once I figured out what direction north was. Or where I was at all, really. I had a lot to do.

Before leaving, I took a moment to steady myself, letting the dim light and lingering murk settle around me. The remnants of old prayers and whispered hopes clung to the walls, a gentle reminder that even in places forgotten by most, someone once cared enough to believe. It seemed almost rude to rush out, so I paused, listening for any sign that The Morrigan might return, but the silence was absolute.

The steel door up the brick stairs opened onto a back alley behind a Chinese restaurant. The dumpster reeked of spoiled vegetables and soured meats, but the end of the alley gave me street signs and a general idea of my location.

Taking the surface streets seemed a little like cheating but I had quite a way to go, and the sun would come up eventually whether I was ready for it or not. The sun is kind of a jerk like that.

My destination was to the north, but the nearest entrance back into the underground was south, under the gymnasium of an elementary school. As entrances go, it wasn't the best but at least it would be closed and presumably unoccupied at night.

I wasn't dressed for surface streets, wearing cargo pants and a tactical vest both loaded with pockets full of ghost hunting electronics, bags of salt and herbs and an objectively unreasonable number of flasks of whiskey, so I moved as quickly as I could without being fast enough to draw attention. This translated to a weird kind of shuffle-walk which sped up or slowed down depending on pedestrian or street traffic and made me look entirely drunk or insane to anyone who was specifically watching me. Fortunately, it seemed like no one was. There are advantages to being in a city and anonymity is one of my favorites. It's just after overlapping public Wi-Fi networks on my list of things I like about urban life.

The elementary school had a locked fence which was basically a formality. I had the decency to put the lock back after I had sprung it. I may have nefarious purposes of my own, but I'm not going to make it easier for anyone with more larcenous intentions.

The gymnasium had a standard lock and an electronic one which I was not equipped to disable, so I picked the mechanical one while I considered my next steps. I had no chance of not triggering the monitored alarm, so I needed to trigger it in a specific way.

I dug through my pockets for a compatible cable for the system and launched an application on my phone.

Part of the physical cyber security initiative that led me to figure out picking locks had covered electronic ones as well. In this case, an underfunded public school, I wasn't surprised to find the default password still in place. I sent the system an overridden time server signal that was thirty-six seconds in the future and slipped inside, pulling the door closed behind me, locking it, and running inside before the program could freak out about the inconsistent clock settings and begin resetting all the sensors and cameras.

The door to the boiler room was behind a folded stand of bleachers that I needed to wheel away from the wall a couple of steps, but I slipped inside and quickly located a grate in the concrete floor.

As I crawled back into the underground, I heard the first notes of the alarm bells, but I knew that it would be dismissed as a software glitch long before anyone would bother to investigate the building itself, if they ever did.

I felt a twinge of guilt about the helpdesk personnel who would be getting calls about the issue but quickly dismissed them. It wasn't my fault the sales engineers had left the default passwords in place.

If a four second Google search can reveal your installation instructions and compromise your whole security system, they were lucky I wasn't there to steal a bunch of whatever elementary schools might have that was worth stealing.

The passage was slick with (I hoped) condensation as I slid along the stone walls before reaching a place where I could stand up again.

This part of the tunnels was older, possibly from mostly being old smuggler's tunnels and certainly not on any of the tourist maps of the official Pedways.

This wasn't on any tours, it wasn't even a shortcut a local might take during harsh weather. It was just me and the damp and whatever old things loved the dark and the deserted places.

Skittering sounds surrounded me, and my narrow flashlight beam just poked temporary holes in the eternal night which surrounded me. Mice? Rats? Spiders the size of mice or rats? Hard claws sliding across damp brick could take any form in my big dumb imagination, and they chose to do so.

The first passageway ended at a tumble of collapsed bricks and stones, so I backtracked to the previous fork and made my way down it. It had been less inviting before but having options removed was a kindness to it this time.

I was tempted again to change my goal towards finding an aboveground exit from the tunnels, to abandon this stupid subterranean journey for a cheap Uber or train ride. But I'm stubborn if you're generous and an idiot if you're a realist, so I pressed on.

This second passage ended in an old cistern, filled with rainwater and clear to the bottom, at least ten feet to the flagstones, but maybe twenty.

The water was lit from the holes in a manhole overhead, so faraway it might as well have been imaginary. I could see a large clay pipe on the opposite wall under the water and could see faint light coming from it. A way out.

Lit only in the very middle from above, the sides of the cistern were cast in darkness so deep my flashlight was useless. Anything could lurk there against the tile-lined walls, waiting for some ghost hunter to enter the water to pounce and end his story there in the watery dark.

I did some brief calculations in my head, the angle of light in the far pipe indicated it wasn't overlong or obstructed, but I was the kind of person who swims to avoid drowning and not for exercise or relaxation. My lungs still burned from time to time from my brush with frostbite and I was still prone to random chest pains even when I was dry and breathing air.

But turning back and finding another lucky path northward was too much of a gamble to risk with the time I had left to make it to where I was going.

With a sigh, I took a plastic bag out of a pocket and began to stuff things into it. Bags of salt, electronics, my phone, every flashlight I carried and bundles of herbs, followed by my socks and pants and flannel, knowing dry clothes on the other side would be important for continued survival if I made it over there alive.

I spent too long pressing the air out of it before sealing it up and fastening it to my waist with my adjustable belt. If it held too much air, it would pull me to the surface at the wrong time and if it leaked and filled with water I would sink like a brick, but I could still admit I was hesitating.

The edges of the cistern were so dark, like an abyss on all sides. There was probably nothing concealed but more water and old tiles, but I couldn't know. Not without going in.

In the end, there was nothing to do but fall in and swim for the exit, so that's what I did.

The water was colder than I had expected, and I had expected it to be very cold. Before I made it to the opening of the pipe, I had stirred up enough silt to blind me. Great ashy clouds of it rose up around me, removing even the artificial sanctuary the light had provided.

Cold began to creep into my fingers and toes first, as though my experience in the frozen Idaho wilderness had made an easy path for it. The rest of me was no slouch though and I started to feel my arms and legs cramp up in rebellion.

I felt the rounded opening of the drainage pipe and pulled myself along the iron handholds on the top of the pipe. I hadn't seen them from above, but I was grateful that someone had thought, decades before, to put them there for future paranormal investigators without the sense the gods granted to goats.

A great cloud of sediment preceded me into the neighboring pool, but I could still see where the light was coming from. Even with that assurance, I was grateful when my head broke the surface, and I took my first breath on the other side.

I quickly broke into wracking coughs, my lungs having had more than enough of the choices I had chosen to make in the too recent past.

Eventually, I pulled myself out of the pool and sprawled across the tile floor. Looking around, I could see another exit heading what I still felt to be vaguely north, but I just lay there on the tile for a while, dripping dry as anyone who has ever tried to pull denim over wet legs knows is a good idea.

Crossing, tile-covered arches spread across the ceiling over me lit by a pale, directionless light from the street.

This had once been a vital public works project, providing drinking water for a fast-growing city overhead. But some decades before, it had been abandoned – replaced by newer infrastructure and promptly forgotten. A lost place, no longer friendly to visitors but carrying on regardless.

I felt a kinship with it and promptly brushed it away.

There was an exit on the north wall, and I had somewhere else to be.

Chapter 10

As I walked, I tried to will my cotton briefs to dry out, but as I still hadn't manifested that particular superpower, or any other for that matter, so I will classify the results as "mixed".

I chafed along another dark hallway, one of countless I had trudged down in the past for reasons I could only guess at now.

My professional life is defined by tangible things – Security settings, best practices, common sense ways of working. It calls my ghost hunting into question, as that is all about chasing the intangible by definition.

Since my excursion into the forests of Idaho I found myself being more reflective. I dearly hoped to figure out why that was before I became too annoying about it.

Unless you happen to be on one of those Travel Channel shows or a member of one of those paranormal investigation groups where everyone wears matching black T-shirts, ghost hunting is a lonely business.

However, in spite of my best efforts and major elements of my personality, I had been gathering a coterie of companions in this endeavor.

I had Lydia, my friend and witchy-fairy-contract-lawyer on speed dial. We lived hours apart but whenever I encountered something that seemed non-ghosty she was who I called.

Ben the werewolf, in Idaho, had taken over his wolfpack when the previous alpha, Isaac, had died on my watch. We didn't talk often, but we traded memes over text. Mostly, I sent him Team Jacob stuff because I'm a jerk but sometimes I'd stray into raw Taylor Lautner territory, and he'd get hit with some Shark boy and Lava girl memes. To be fair, he sent a lot of Big Bang Theory memes in response, which told me I should really learn how to explain my job better to people who have my phone number.

I doubt Ben would drive or fly down to help me out in a pinch, but I knew that the issue was mostly logistics. By the time I needed the help of a pack of werewolves, they were too far away to make a difference. He would be there for me if it was possible, because we had traded stories and the promise of more of them was too much to ignore.

But my first companion had been Meghan, and she had died on a ghost hunt with me, which left me with unfathomable depths of guilt and feelings of being not up to the task.

Imposter syndrome, thy name is Lawrence Miller.

Bright, white lights flickered against the walls ahead of me a few steps before I started to hear muffled voices. The clatter of equipment and the faint hum of electronics grew as I continued down the tunnel.

I was grateful for all the noise these people were making as I paused in the shadow of a corner in the passageway so I could listen in on whatever was going on down there in the supposedly abandoned dark.

"The Phantom Files audience demands that we put ourselves out there," a nasally voice announced, "So one of you needs to crawl down that shaft and report the findings."

"Eat shit, Doug," a woman answered, "That's a ventilation shaft and there's no way to know where it ends up."

"No way unless you crawl down it," someone apparently named Doug replied, "I'll keep one camera on your face for dramatic effect and another to follow your descent. The audience will love it."

"We have thousands of dollars in cameras here," the woman sighed, "Lower one of those and see of the tunnel pinches off or ends in water or a pile of rats or something."

"Rats don't form piles," a third voice, a man, offered, "They don't congregate in that form, it's typically more of a tangle – little vertical action at all, really."

"Shut up, Lloyd," both other voices answered in stereo, in a way which suggested they had had a good deal of practice.

"Sometimes the tails get all tangled and they form something called a 'rat king', but eventually they pull against each other long enough to just starve to death," Lloyd muscled on, ignoring his companions.

It says something about me that this immediately made him my favorite, whatever that was worth.

"I am not going into that tunnel, headfirst or otherwise," the woman proclaimed, "and our fans can just deal with it."

"Do you want them calling us cowards, Britney?" Doug asked.

"I don't want then calling us at all, Doug," apparently Britney said, "But I'd appreciate it if they'd shower before the Sunday meet and greet at next year's ParaNormaCon."

"Weekend events are long," Lloyd offered, "and there are objectively a lot of activities and panels to attend."

"This is why we pack a hygiene kit for you," Doug explained, "We love you, man, but your laser-focus doesn't leave a lot of room for olfactory considerations."

"The ladies love the LEDs," Lloyd smirked, "They don't care so much about anything after a fully formed apparition wanders down a hallway in full HD."

I then decided that I hated all of them, but the order in which I hated them was shuffling like someone offering three-card Monty in front of Union Station. I respected the game, but I had contempt for the players. And the fact that I had been within a few feet of them long enough to hear all of this made it even more egregious. If these people were really investigating the paranormal with this little situational awareness, they were eventually going to get themselves killed, and I had experienced more than enough of that already.

The three exchanged glances, their faces illuminated in stark, unnatural highlights by the harsh lights of their equipment. Nervous energy bounced between them, the silence stretching just a beat too long as each seemed to wait for someone else to speak first. For a second, it was almost comical. Ghost hunters more afraid of a living person leaving them a bad review than any spirit lurking in the shadows.

I stomped my feet a few times before stepping around the corner with my hands up, partially to show I wasn't armed but mostly to shield my eyes from the glare of the camera lamps. How these people expected to see anything in the dark while constantly spoiling their night vision was a mystery to me.

"Who are you guys?" I pretended to know less than I did, which wasn't hard even though I didn't know much, "Travel Channel? History? Bravo?"

Even after telegraphing my appearance, all three of them jumped, startled into bewildered and frustrating inaction.

"C-Span?"

"Who the hell are you?" the one named Doug asked. He was tall and lanky, wearing cargo pants and one of those cool tactical sweaters [GP3] with the solid patch of matching fabric sewn to the shoulder, like some European Special Forces extra in a 90s action movie. Or even an 80's Christmas movie like Die Hard.

For the record, he couldn't pull it off.

"Lawrence Miller," I answered, "and I'm just passing through."

"Nobody just passes through here, dude," Britney scoffed, blonde ponytail bouncing behind the safety goggles perched on her head.

"Yeah," I sighed, "I got turned around. I'm just headed north towards the river now, so I'll leave you to," I gestured vaguely at everything, "whatever the hell it is you guys are doing."

"We're filming a documentary series about paranormal Chicago," Doug gestured at me with his camera, "You may have heard of the Phantom Files?"

"I don't watch a lot of TV," I lied. I watch plenty, mostly travel series or something where somebody has to fix up old broken things. Paranormal "reality" television is dumb at best and dangerous at worst, as it encouraged idiots like these to go into increasingly dangerous situations.

"Maybe you've heard of a little website called YouTube?" Lloyd mocked.

"Shut up, Lloyd," again, in stereo. It was uncanny.

"You're all down here in the abandoned bad parts of the Chicago underground for some YouTube show?" I was honestly surprised, but I shouldn't have been. Some of those creators make some serious money.

"It's a top YouTube show," Britney attempted to clarify.

“Please tell me you’re all up to date on your tetanus shots,” I shook my head, “Honestly if you all didn’t look too old to still live at home, I’d call your mothers.”

Lloyd shuffled a little bit, his Crocs digging fresh furrows in the dust on the floor.

“Maybe not all of you,” I amended, shrugging.

“We know what we’re doing,” Doug sneered, “You’re the one with no idea what you are wandering around in.”

“Prohibition smuggling tunnels, old water works and electrical maintenance shafts?” I gestured again, “I’ve crawled through worse. And more sober.”

Lloyd giggled a little insanely, and slapped Britney on the shoulder with the back of his hand, “He doesn’t know he’s walking around the basement of the Chicago Murder Castle.”

Chapter 11

Prohibition is synonymous with Chicago. While it was a national ban on alcoholic beverages, some of the most famous resistance was in and around Chicago.

Organized crime existed before bootlegging became commonplace, but illegal drink became a profit center for it, not only boosting revenue in the short-term but establishing vast amounts of generational wealth for some families that allowed them to branch out into new and exciting crimes when booze was again legalized.

Including, eventually, the presidency.

One of my favorite terrible reminders of our brief return to puritanical alcohol standards is a local Chicago liquor, Jeppson's Malört.

The story goes that a Swedish immigrant wanted to recreate a digestif from his homeland, only he didn't have the recipe and decades of cigar smoking had ruined his ability to taste anything, so a traditional wormwood drink became horrifically amplified in flavor in Chicago.

According to legend, he was allowed to sell his booze as medicinal throughout the prohibition era, because it tasted so horrible no one could believe anyone would drink it recreationally.

You can still buy it in plenty of local bars, and it has spread across the continent, the perfect drink to encapsulate the self-loathing that defines a good and proper bender.

Malört is a rite of passage in Chicago pubs, to the point that the easiest way to get a free drink in the entire world is to walk into a Chicago bar, point at a bottle and say, "Jeppson's Malört? What's that?"

It's a unique marketing strategy based not on creating a product that people enjoy, but on making one so terrible that people want to inflict it on friends and loved ones. It probably won't kill them, but until they get the taste of it out of their mouth, they may truly wish that it had.

I personally have inflicted it on friends and coworkers numerous times, drinking it myself with them because of all the ways that I may be a monster, dodging the Malört I am inflicting on others isn't one of them.

I don't know how it is made, but my assumption has always been that the Swedes with their endless winter nights discovered a way to distill clinical depression and then filter it through a dirty gym sock soaked in Vick's VapoRub. Then they justifiably exiled the inventor to Chicago where he fell victim to the same gypsy curse that made the Cubs suck for decades.

If you'd like to make your own version at home, push a lawnmower through an abandoned herb garden and then filter the contents of the bag, bugs and all, through a tire fire and then just distill the results.

Or just buy a bottle. It's appropriately cheap and discourages visitors in a way that a large and aggressive or even especially flatulent dog can only envy.

Some horrors aren't paranormal at all, I guess. Some can just taste like you've squeezed a shrub soaked in kerosine through your teeth and lit it on fire while it went down.

In short: Four stars, would recommend.

Chapter 12

As I looked around the cracked brickwork and as far as I could see down the corridors which snaked away from the little room we were all crowded into, my brain tried to reconcile what I knew about the geography and history above with where I stood.

The Chicago Murder Castle had been torn down decades earlier and replaced with nothing. An empty lot sits between a post office and the elevated rail line, prime real estate left empty because no one living can be comfortable long in a place which was famously a home for the dead or the soon to be. It still gets visitors, mostly history buffs or true crime enthusiasts. More than a few ghost hunting teams have wandered across the grass over the years.

There's no monument or marker, but the site is plainly different than the rest of the Englewood neighborhood. It's still healing, I hope.

H.H. Holmes had spent his life murdering people and gathering their wealth, adding it to his own until he could build a hotel and apartments three miles from the site of the World's Fair. He marketed it as a place for fair goers from out of town to stay, but checking out was never guaranteed.

There are some fun conspiracy theories suggesting that before his Chicago adventures, H.H. Holmes used his medical background to sow terror in London as the unindicted perpetrator of the Jack the Ripper murders.

Constructed with a warren of secret rooms, ancient sound-proofing and hidden passageways, the interior was never fully mapped out. America's first official serial killer tortured and murdered his guests here and disposed of their remains underground. Possibly passing through this area on his way or burying them right under where we stood.

As someone who spends a problematic amount of time actively seeking out haunted places, this was still tangibly creepy. Even being this close to such a monumental amount of human suffering took a toll on me.

"Why the hell are you guys under the murder castle?" I asked.

"Our viewers expect us to go into the most haunted places," Doug started, "and the Chicago Murder Castle was at the top of the list on our latest online poll."

"Okay," I chuckled, "Great, but those are wildly inaccurate and there are at least a dozen haunted places in Chicago which are less dangerous than the underground beneath the freaking murder castle."

"Oh," Britney interjected, "Like the haunted Hooter's?"

"The haunted Hooter's is across the river from here," I admitted, "and their wings are not the best."

"We get paid for clicks and views and our subscribers wanted the murder castle, and the Phantom Files always delivers," Doug proclaimed.

"I admire your dedication," I had obviously developed an allergy to telling the truth, "But if this place is actually haunted, it is the dangerous kind of haunted. You're out of your depth."

"We are professionals," Lloyd answered, "we've been in a lot of haunted places."

"We have some of the best recorded evidence you can find on YouTube," Britney agreed, "Have you seen the clip with the axe head in Mineral Wells?"

I had, but clicking on the terms and conditions for viewing the video didn't include admitting it in sub-surface Chicago.

"The Mineral Wells, Texas house across from the mortuary? Down the road from the Crazy Water Hotel?"

"That's the one!" Doug spat, "We were there!"

I had investigated the same property years before and it had every reason to be haunted.

Built as a family house in the 1800s, it had been devastated by disease at first. Then one of the children was abducted by the local Native American tribe, resulting in the return of the child and the beheading of the perpetrator in the front yard.

The house was eventually sold and repurposed as a brothel for years while the Crazy Water Hotel operated right down the street. Legend tells that one of the ladies gave birth to a child with some deformity who was left in the attic to live or die as nature demanded.

I personally spent five hours in that attic trying to make contact with any entity that was consigned there to the dark. It was before the house got remodeled and marketed for paranormal groups to visit.

"Did you talk about the spring water that ran under the hotel and then under the mortuary and the house itself?" I asked.

"We couldn't investigate the hotel," Lloyd admitted.

"No," I slashed with my hand, "Not the hotel where the Three Stooges relaxed back in the day. Did you look into the water?"

"Why would we look into the water?" Doug asked, "Our viewers expect apparitions, and we deliver those."

"The medicinal spring water of the Crazy Water Hotel Spa," I elaborated, "contains magnesium and iron and lithium."

"So?" Britany asked, "It's just water."

"Lithium is an antipsychotic," I tried to keep my voice out of a sing-song mocking tone but honestly, I didn't try really hard, "unless you're already given to delusions, or especially if you aren't, in which case results are all across the spectrum."

"Are you suggesting," Lloyd asked, "That the evidence from our investigation were the results of something in the water?"

"No," I shook my head, already convinced but looking for a way to talk about anything else, "I'm suggesting that you guys are going to get killed down here and I'm actively trying to not touch anything, so the FBI won't have questions for me later."

"We investigated Alcatraz," Doug started, "and Gettysburg and Eastern State Penitentiary in Pennsylvania. We know what we're doing."

"You went to famously haunted places with crowds of other enthusiasts with fancy electronics."

"We got plenty of good evidence," Lloyd defended.

"Yeah," I nodded, "everyone does. It's low-hanging paranormal fruit. But what happens when a ghost tries to murder you?"

"Ghosts aren't physically aggressive," Lloyd explained, "They toss things around a little and make temperature shifts and weird noises, but they can't hurt you."

I pictured the smoking hole in Meghan's chest, put there by a ghost, and wondered briefly how much the earlier encounter with her doppelganger was affecting me.

"You are the one that can't be here," Doug announced, "We don't have time to babysit some tourist."

"Fine," I agreed, "You don't have to babysit me. I'll be on my way once you answer one question for me."

"What's that?" Doug asked.

"Where the hell did Britney go?"

Chapter 13

We could all agree that she had just been right there. She had valid and current input for the conversation. At some point, though, she just hadn't been there anymore.

Doug shined a flashlight down the ventilation shaft she had earlier refused to crawl down while Lloyd and I took several steps down each corridor, yelling after her and hoping for a response. We never heard one.

When we returned to the central room, Doug was calling Britney on his cellphone without getting an answer. I couldn't hear any ringing so if she had her phone with her, she was too far away.

My own cell signal was fine, so we weren't that deep underground. I had a missed call from Lydia and three from some unknown government agency, probably Agents Smith and Jones attempting to find out where I was or, because they probably knew that already, to add something to my to-do list.

I might someday answer an unknown caller if I was lost in the wilderness and trapped under a fallen tree, but it wouldn't be happening while I was a couple of dozen feet under the third largest city in the country. Even if the sauce was on top of their weirdly thick pizza like the fundamental rules of food don't matter. It's delicious, Chicago, but that doesn't make it okay.

I've lived alone long enough that I have a rule about emergency calls. Anyone that knows me knows that I won't spend more than twenty minutes in a grocery store. If I can't find what I'm looking for, there's no one who is going to complain about that back home, so if I've been in the store for more than half an hour or so, someone should call the paramedics because obviously a giant cooler full of frozen pizza has fallen on me and I can't escape. Or chew my own leg off. I really hate shopping for food.

I also really hate responding to voicemail, so my outgoing message is still the default robotic lady voice just stating my phone number and I've never checked the messages. I just feel weird giving people the illusion that I will put any priority on calling them back when I have no idea why they called me in the first place.

But Britney was gone and that was the immediate problem.

"Could she have gone somewhere on purpose?" I asked, "Where is your base for this investigation? Does it have a restroom?"

"You have no idea how ghost hunts work, guy," Doug sighed, "We have a process, and Britney knows it."

I turned my head so no one could see my eyes involuntarily examine the inside of the top of my skull. I've been in enough weekly project status meetings to make that particular flinch instinctive.

"Great," I offered, "What happens in your process when someone on your team disappears in the middle of an investigation?"

The silence I was answered with was expected, but I wasn't especially comforted by it.

The catacombs we were in smelled like stale dust and damp and canceled plans. Whole lives of canceled plans. It was overpowering to the point where I almost missed the thin current of moving air heading vaguely north but definitely upward. Something warm was below us and the scents of the deeper dark were being carried past us on their gentle way towards the streets above.

I dug around my pockets and produced a plastic bag filled with dried herbs and thrust it at Lloyd, "Hang on to this for a second," before digging around further. I handed a couple of spare flashlights to Doug who needed to adjust his grip on his camera as I turned to hand a small rechargeable headlamp to Lloyd.

I held out a full flask of whiskey and then tucked it away again before depositing a handful of change to both of them along with another bundle of herbs, a piece of chalk, and a paper bag filled with miraculously still-dry salt.

"We need to find your friend and I can't do that with disorganized pockets," I explained, taking items back one by one and putting them back exactly from where I'd gotten them. The whole process had happened quickly enough that Lloyd and Doug had remained speechless until I took back the final items I had handed to each of them.

"Why are you carrying rusty nails?" Doug asked.

"Better to have them and not need them," my smile tight as I reached out to reclaim both nails.

I still hadn't figured out a legitimate witchy use for rusty nails in my day-to-day paranormal excursions, but I knew the iron in them would have hurt a Fae creature who touched them, at least enough to spoil the illusion of a human form, so I could be sure these guys were most likely human.

It made me able to turn my back to them and move down the dark corridor into the deeper places of sub-Chicago, flashlight leading the way.

I counted about ten paces before I heard Lloyd and Doug following hesitantly after me, their own lamps flashing along the bricks ahead.

Chapter 14

A few hundred feet down the corridor from where we had started, I saw a swirled pattern of disturbed dust in the concrete in front of a dark opening in the brick wall. A quick glance told me that this was an old, improvised opening in a ventilation shaft from a much deeper and older section of tunnels.

Mildewed, damp air rose through the stone tunnel and escaped through the hole in front of me, washing over me like a breeze through a graveyard. Like the last, cold breath of a drowning man.

My flashlight illuminated a line of rusted metal rungs bricked into the far wall of the tube, reachable from the side I was on but on the other side of a plunge deep enough that my light couldn't find the bottom. The darkness seemed to absorb the light, reflecting nothing at all past the first half dozen steps down.

Flipping the flashlight, I could only see up a few feet before the vertical ascent was blocked by a tangle of fallen timbers. That way had been cut off and impassable for a while judging by the thick, dust-choked cobwebs stretched across the rough-cut wood.

Lloyd and Doug peered over my shoulders into the dark for a moment, the three of us hoping to see some sign of Britney almost as much as we were hoping to see nothing else down there in the dark.

"You think she went down there?" Doug asked, "She wouldn't go down the other vent with climbing gear and a helmet light, but she'd just climb down this one on her own?"

"I don't know how ghost hunting on YouTube works," I started, "but anyone who wants to make a career out of paranormal investigation can't be counted on to make the best decisions."

"We should call the police," Lloyd offered.

"Yeah," I nodded, "You do that and lead them here. You're on your own for explaining why you're out of the pedestrian areas of the tunnels hours after they close down for the night."

I took out my own phone and fired off a quick text to Smith and Jones wherever they were and another to Lydia in Austin, doing my best to guess at where I was with a quick line about crawling down farther into the darkness before dropping the phone back into a pocket so that I could grip the crumbling brick work with both hands.

"But whatever you do," I said over my shoulder, "don't follow me. I'll find Britney or she can't be found."

"We can help," Doug objected, "This isn't our first ghost hunt."

I rolled my eyes futilely in the dark before saying, "I'm not babysitting two grown men and this isn't a ghost hunt, anymore. It's a hunt for a person I very much hope is still alive."

"The ghost hunt never totally stops," Lloyd said, "It's all around us all the time."

"Let's hope it isn't around Britney," I sighed, taking a length of rope from the side of Doug's backpack and slinging the loop over my shoulder.

"We'll wait here," Doug said, not protesting my borrowing his rope at all, "Call out if you need help."

"Just alert emergency services and try to figure out where the hell we are," I leaned out over the abyss and tried to touch the ladder on the far side, but I hadn't reached far enough before I dislodged a rain of brick dust which clattered and fell down into the hole.

"What if he has her?" Lloyd asked quietly, "What if the ghost of H.H. Holmes has her?"

I swung by one arm across the vent and gripped the closest rusty metal rung, using it to pull myself across.

"Shut up, Lloyd," I said at the same time as Doug. Maybe that trick didn't require as much practice as I had assumed it would.

I couldn't see far enough down into the dark to see my own feet, so I lowered myself by feel. Rung by rung I descended, eventually shutting off my flashlight to conserve battery life when it wasn't doing anything but making me a beacon in the dark.

There is a quality to places which are out of the reach of sunlight. It's not always unwholesome, but it often is.

I've spent time in caves and abandoned storm shelters, windowless attics and once even the tunnels surrounding a decommissioned missile silo in Nebraska, the whole thing sprawling under a blighted cornfield long gone feral overhead, and each of those places had that quality tempered with just enough humanity to make it a claimed space for the living.

As I went deeper and deeper into a place which would make even eternal night feel like a tanning bed, that thread of humanity became more and more frayed and all wholesomeness faded away into the endless shadows.

My feet found the debris-cluttered flagstone floor and I switched the flashlight back on to check for signs of recent passage as well as to make note of the exits from the base of the vent.

I couldn't see light from above even though I didn't think Doug and Lloyd had wandered off. It was possibly too far, or maybe the shaft had imperceptibly twisted too far for line of sight.

A broken brick had been knocked over recently enough to leave an obvious dust-free patch on the floor in front of a steel-ringed exit portal to my left.

I checked my pockets again, compulsively, and verified that my phone had no signal this far underground even though I knew that it wouldn't.

As I stepped over the rim of the passage and passed from darkness into more darkness, a male voice giggled in the endless night behind me.

Chapter 15

If I hadn't been delayed by detours and missing YouTube dancing monkeys, I might have found myself under The Nederlander Theatre downtown. It's a home for regional productions as well as touring Broadway shows and boasts state-of-the-art light and sound facilities. The Nederlander is a must-see for patrons of the arts or people on third dates who have exhausted ax throwing and escape rooms as options.

It also burned down to the façade in 1903 when it was still called The Iroquois Theatre after being advertised as fire-proof. Nine years before the reportedly unsinkable Titanic navigated to the bottom of the Atlantic, The Iroquois Theatre burned itself out partially due to the intended fireproofing.

During a matinee, a blue-tinted spotlight ignited a muslin curtain and the fire raced for the roof too quickly to be extinguished. It quickly reached several thousand yards of oil painted backdrops hung from the rafters and even modern firefighting technology would be hard-pressed to stop things after that.

The expensive asbestos fire curtain got hung up on a light fixture before it could effectively seal off the proscenium arch and backstage from the crowd, but inspectors later testified that what was supposed to be asbestos was mostly wood pulp and of no use at all in preventing a fire from spreading.

All of this was just fine according to the fire codes of the time, but it was later alleged that fire inspectors were regularly bribed with free tickets, anyway.

Eddie Foy, who was playing the character of "Sister Anne" in the burlesque was later quoted as saying that during the first act, looking over the crowd, he had never seen so many women and children in a theatre crowd before. Whole families were in attendance, even in the gallery seating.

He attempted to keep the crowd calm while the roof burst into flames and huge pieces of flaming scenery crashed down around him.

Good luck convincing me drag brunches are a bad thing.

The smoke doors on the roof had been sealed shut at some point, so the smoke tried to escape through the same exits the patrons did, and smoke can carry on without oxygen a lot longer than human lungs can.

There were thirty exits for the audience to use in the event of a fire, but most opened inwards resulting in a crush of people holding them shut and others employing a European-style latch which was frustratingly unfamiliar to an American audience. Most of the exits were covered with drapes and unmarked, too, so only three exit doors were ever opened on the audience side. And one of those may have been blown open by the explosion of a huge fireball from backstage.

There were no fire alarms and no way to call the fire department, so trucks weren't dispatched until smoke was sighted.

In the end, the alley behind the theatre served as a makeshift morgue for the over six-hundred dead, mostly audience members, and fire codes were re-written locally to require that exit doors be marked and open outwards.

172 students would have to die in the Collinwood School Fire in Ohio in 1908 for those requirements to be adopted nationally.

The building has been replaced, but the tunnels still connect to it.

The first reporter to break the story saw a "knight and three elves" crawling out of a manhole, actors fleeing the fire through a backstage exit, and built a whole career out of reporting around the investigation of the fire and the political and criminal downfalls of the responsible parties.

But none of that can help the dead, who reportedly still show up in that alley, since renamed "Couch Place".

People report apparitions, the faint sounds of crying, and feelings of being touched or shoved when visiting which has given "Couch Place" the nickname "Death Alley".

Chapter 16

I couldn't see the source of the giggling, so I did my best to ignore it as I went deeper into the underground. There's a space in my brain where I tend to stash things I can't do anything about.

At the time, that space was crowded already with whatever it was the Fae were planning, the price of The Morrigan's protection, Climate Change and the status of more than a few of my personal relationships.

But the giggling didn't stop or even change into a chuckle or an outright laugh at any point. Just a deep, male voice giggling in the darkness around me, from in front of me as well as behind.

Every ten steps or so I drew a chalk arrow on the wall to my right because the only thing worse than not finding Britney would be finding her and then both of us being lost under Chicago forever.

I didn't have any concerns that the giggling ghost would erase the marks. Most ghosts don't notice if you've added a door or stairwell since they died. They just pass through walls or disappear when confronted with new construction, so a chalk mark on a wall would be entirely off the radar for a typical ghost.

I was a little relieved to be followed by a ghost, as the past few months had been consumed by zombies and werewolves and ancient Jewish mystical monsters. Ghosts I could handle. Almost comfort food at this point, ghosts are the macaroni and cheese of the damned for a paranormal investigator.

A fresh, textured shoe print told me the way Britney had gone, so I dutifully followed after. I hadn't seen more than a single type of print, so I was reasonably certain that Britney was alone down here. No living person had abducted her from where she and her friends and I had been talking, which led me to wonder why she would take off on her own and head into a space which was definitely more perilous than the one she had declined to be lowered into earlier.

Something was off, and whatever personal Spidey Sense I could point at and admit was real was screaming at me to consider my next steps much more carefully.

I tripped over a concrete ledge that had looked like just another shadow on the floor and tried to catch myself with the arm I had bruised running from the long-dead Nazi U-boat captain. I failed miserably, landing in an ungraceful heap on the dusty cement.

Soft giggling echoed around me as I laid there. Sometimes in life we are confronted with moments which test our self-esteem, and very often those moments pile up on us like the universe's prosecutor showing evidence to a jury who you just hope at the end of the day takes a little bit of pity on you.

The other sounds started so softly that I felt them through the rubber soles of my shoes before I heard them, a pulse-like noise, rhythmic and insistent, pulling me forward in spite of being completely unappealing.

The lights followed soon after, strobing white around a distant corner and blue and red peppered generously with the soft purple of blacklight, all following the bass line of what was probably technically music by generous definitions.

Chicago has a famous underground rave scene, but the largest provider has over a hundred thousand members on their social media pages so it's not as "underground" as it used to be, and it isn't as "underground" as the pop-up events in the tunnels beneath downtown. The only way to score an invitation to one of those is to know someone who is already invited, and Facebook is absolutely not the place where the details are solidified.

I knew if Britney had come this way, other mortal humans could guide her back to the surface. But I wasn't certain that she had. My tracking skills are rusty and the last time I used them it was to identify tracks in wet sand made by a plastic animal paw as part of a merit badge experience, all twelve of us cub scouts authoritatively yelling about the differences between fox tracks and those from a coyote as if any of us had seen either animal outside of a zoo, ever. But I hadn't seen any disturbances in the dust off of the trail I was following, so I would need to settle for Best Guess Territory. I'm a frequent flier there, though, so the discomfort was negligible. The emotional baggage fees tend to pile up in a way which occasionally feels like a personal attack, but I don't have a frame of reference to contest it.

The weird masculine giggling faded into the background as I turned the final corner and encountered the sub-street party.

I don't want to come off as old or ancient or hopelessly out of touch, but the scene before me had other ideas about my perceptions and the delusional bouncers were ill-equipped to keep me out of anything.

Hey, let me shorthand this for anyone who wants to get as close as possible to the stage at any concert ever.

Do this:

Buy two over-priced drinks at the approved vendor station. In my case, this is whiskey, but the only limit is your imagination. Buy two of whatever and then hold them proudly in front of you, as sacred talismans.

Thrust yourself forward, drinks in front of you, through the crowd. Know that they will part for you. Their whole purpose is in enjoying the vibe of the audience and they assume you're bringing a drink to a friend up near the stage. Or at least they'll get out of the way to avoid getting that drink spilled on them. Either way, you've got a straight shot to the area next to the stage that you only paid for a single extra drink for and, at least in my case, you intended to drink that anyway.

It may not still work that way. I will admit it has been more than a minute since I needed front row access for live music so perhaps things have changed. Your mileage may vary, I guess.

But when I turned the final corner, I realized that things had not changed enough to make any difference.

Black lights and neon in weird strips covered the attendants and whatever music was playing was overwhelmed by powerful bass lines, disorienting and putting my senses into turmoil.

The tangle of dancers in the strobing lights before me were cognitively dissonant. I could process vignettes individually, if I kept my neck stationary, but I did not, so the fluorescent swirl was overpowering in the thick sound of the rave before me.

When I was in high school and, to be honest, college, most of my social interactions involved Dungeons and Dragons or, if the cool kids were involved, the boardgame Risk as a drinking game.

If you've never had to take a shot of vodka when your Kamchatka was conquered, I will generously forgive you for not being aware of the pain involved in that loss. But a tunnel rave in Chicago has different rules. Or possibly no rules at all.

I won't pretend I saw things that I'd never seen before, but I will freely tell you that I had never seen them accidentally and, more importantly, that I hadn't seen them when I was just trying to navigate some restricted and probably haunted subterranean tunnels in an ill-advised attempt to rescue some YouTube personality.

I saw Britney step past the bouncer to exit the whole rave and followed after her. I was more than a little grateful to have come at this event from a direction which hadn't involved my identification.

I moved through the crowd to follow her, but noted that I was followed from the underground by a grinning, tweed-coated man with a thick mustache.

He followed behind me, weaving and ducking between the gyrating participants of the impromptu dance party here in this abandoned section of tunnel.

Apart from the mustache, his apparent age and dated dress he was indistinguishable from the rest of the crowd. He was tangible and notably watching me in my pursuit.

On his trip towards the front of the stage people seemed to shy away from him instinctively. Our gut reactions are hard-coded, the result of millions of years of evolution. Only idiots ignore them, and they don't survive to pass on their genomes most of the time. Thankfully.

We, that is to say mortal humans, have defense mechanisms which limit our engagement with the inconceivable. We grow filters which inform us of nonsense, and we use a lot of mental resources to do so.

And if you stick to normal human activities there isn't a lot of impact from this. If you've created a life out of not chasing the darkness into weird, haunted places or spots which your fellow humans have decided are off limits, you can possibly spend an entire life leaning into ignoring your gut instincts, but I don't know. I chase that stuff, so I'm hardly the authority on what regular people would do.

One person lacked that instinct and, clad in tan pants and a V-necked green shirt, he chose to step towards my pursuer and obstruct his path for part of a second.

The mustached man lightly laid a hand on his shoulder and lights flashed in the strobing chaos of the dancefloor.

The rave participant in the green shirt collapsed to the floor as though all bones had been teleported out of him. Anything that made him a person was just gone. The brief flash of light was enough for me to identify the process, but none of that mattered as it blended to near invisibility, drowned out by the multicolored strobes around us.

The man with the mustache didn't even bother to watch him fall. His gaze was on me, and he kept watching as I edged past the bouncer and followed Britney into more darkness.

Chapter 17

A little over three years after the Titanic sank into the freezing waters of the Atlantic, enough time had passed for meaningful legislation and updated regulations to have been enacted to improve the safety of passengers and crews on maritime voyages.

One specific boat designed to haul fruit at twenty-two miles an hour so it would stay fresh on the way to market, was sold and repurposed several times since it hit the water of the Great Lakes. It sat too low in the water initially, so the coal engines were moved higher and the hardwood decks in the front were replaced with concrete to decrease the part of the ship that sat beneath the waterline.

The SS Eastland, a steamship on the Chicago River, had enough lifeboats, per post-Titanic regulation, to accommodate everyone in the event of an emergency. Unfortunately, there were also enough lifeboats to make the Eastland top heavy. It capsized violently, trapping people below decks and battering them with heavy furniture designed to remain stationary through moderate weather but transformed to crushing projectiles when the boat flipped suddenly.

What had started as an outing to a mandatory employee picnic ended a few hours later with the deadliest event in Great Lakes maritime history before even leaving the dock, with most of the dead being immigrant workers from Norway, Germany, Poland, Ireland, Denmark, Italy and Hungary with over two-hundred dead just from what is now the Czech Republic.

Rescue efforts eventually gave way to recovery ones and businesses along what is now the famous Chicago Riverwalk were used as makeshift trauma centers and then morgues as more and more bodies were pulled out of the wreckage and the water. In total, 843 people, mostly passengers, lost their lives in the Eastland disaster.

The incident cast a harsh light on the treatment of America's immigrant workforce with Carl Sandburg writing in "The *Eastland*",

"I see a dozen *Eastlands*

Every morning on my way to work

And a dozen more going home at night".

The poem was too inflammatory to see print in 1915 but appeared in a collection in an anthology almost eight decades later.

The ship was salvaged, sold to the navy, and used as a training vessel through World War II after being renamed the USS Wilmette. It even carried FDR on a 10-day fishing excursion in 1943 before eventually being decommissioned and then scrapped in 1947.

Tragedy marks a place in a way that even flowing water can't erode over time, and the Eastland disaster is no different.

People report apparitions along the shoreline, strange waves and water patterns in the river and ghostly voices crying out in foreign languages all along the riverwalk.

Chapter 18

Britney darted down the ink-black corridor so quickly that I had to call out a few times to catch her attention and convince her to wait for me.

We passed an old freight elevator which had likely deposited the partygoers down here for the illicit dance party but too quickly for me to guess at where it might lead.

"Hey," I started, "Britney, I've got to get you back to your weird YouTube friends and it is very important that we not wander around down here,"

"Who died and made you Batman?" she asked, turning to face me, "Oh, wait. Was it your parents? Because if it was your parents, please forgive my interjection, Mister Wayne."

I was at a loss for words, which is about as uncomfortable as I can physically be.

I've had frostbite. I have had a number of ball and socket joints pulled out of function. An arm or leg free from fresh scabs is kind of a novelty for me. But still.

"Take it up with Alfred, Britney," I grunted, grabbing her elbow and dragging her towards what I only hoped was the surface.

Checking behind me for the guy with the mustache was a reflex. As a ghost, he could just as easily be in front of us. I was relying on one constant trait of the dead – They pretend they have to play by the same rules the living follow.

Maybe it is a comfort to them, some familiarity or even just habit. The same defect that makes them ignore recent construction makes them pretend to have to follow the same rules of physics that govern our universe.

Until they don't.

Eventually, a ghost following the rules of living will get frustrated enough to realize that they can make their own rules. And that's when the gloves come off and things get weird.

We were on a clock that we weren't allowed to look at and when that countdown hit zero, things were going to go horribly wrong, and I needed to have Britney handed off and be a distant memory for the YouTube set when that happened.

I wasn't ready to be the last known survivor of another paranormal incident. This was supposed to be a very simple, ghosty weekend.

Honestly, by now a "simple ghosty weekend" should send me packing for the hills the same way as "Hot singles in your area" or "I just need access to an Americanese bank account to process my funds as a Nigerian Prince", but while I make bad decisions quickly, ghosty weekends are also kind of my whole thing. And it's important to have a hobby.

"I think somebody just died back there and if we don't keep moving, we might be next," I tugged her forward, "What the hell are you doing taking off down here alone anyway?"

She looked puzzled for a second before shaking her head as if to clear it, "I don't remember."

"What are you, drunk?" I asked, "Did you take some weird club drug back there?"

"No," at least she had the sense to keep moving, "It just seemed like the thing to do, I guess."

Back when I hunted ghosts in larger groups, I experienced the same phenomenon.

Otherwise level-headed and reasonable investigators would take bizarre actions or make dangerous decisions, always later reporting that it had felt like a good idea at the time.

"I have it on good authority that the ghost around here is a very dangerous one," I offered.

"You don't actually believe in ghosts, do you?" she asked incredulously.

"I'm not the one who makes a living putting paranormal investigations on the internet!" I was a little offended.

I mean, I'm an information security consultant, so making money off people's fears isn't completely unfamiliar territory for me.

"Doug is the true believer, and Lloyd just likes the attention," Britney shrugged, "The mouth breathers who watch our show mostly do it to watch me run around in infrared in a t-shirt, judging from the comment section."

"As much as I hate all of that, Doug and Lloyd are up top waiting for us," I answered, "and I'd rather get to them before they send first responders down here."

"Do you even know the way out?" she asked.

"I'm a tourist," I admitted, "but I'm used to being tourist. We will find our own way out."

I couldn't hear the dull thrum of the music behind us anymore, but I couldn't say whether it was simple distance or if the DJ had paused the audio assault because the collapsed partygoer in the green shirt had been hopefully noticed by someone. And helped, if there was anything to be done.

Britney cast a glance over her shoulder, unease flickering briefly across her face before she got control of her expression. The passage ahead sloped upward, the concrete walls narrowing as if the tunnel itself were intent on herding us toward our inevitable fate. My phone's flashlight cast strange shadows, elongating our figures and revealing the faded remnants of graffiti, messages from previous explorers or perhaps warnings we were too late to heed. I'd have loved to have seen my earlier navigation chalk marks among them.

We stepped carefully, our footsteps muffled by a fine layer of dust and party debris. Somewhere behind, the faint echo of voices drifted over us, distorted, remote, reminding us that life continued elsewhere, untouched by the tangles of the underground. Britney stopped at an intersection, her gaze darting between three branching corridors.

"Left, right, or straight?" she asked, voice low but steady.

I hesitated. "Logic says left. Gut says straight. But I'm open to democratic process if you're feeling brave."

She snorted. "Democracy in the abandoned underground. What could go wrong?"

We chose straight, plunging further into the gloom. Here, the air grew heavier, close and damp, each breath tinged with the memory of mold and old machinery. My mind wandered to Doug and Lloyd, picturing them above us, eager for the next thrill, impatient to stage another moment for their eager viewers. I wondered, not for the first time, who the real ghouls were. The restless dead, or those of us drawn to stories of those who refused or were unable to rest?

A sudden scuffle behind us made us both spin, hearts thudding with the possibility of death or disaster. For an instant, I thought I saw a movement, a shadow darting just out of range of the light. But when I focused, there was nothing there except a half-crushed plastic cup and the errant shimmer of dust motes.

Britney smiled, thin and crooked. "Maybe your stupid ghost wants us to get lost."

"Or maybe it's hoping you'll find something worth broadcasting," I snarked, pressing forward, feeling the weight of curiosity, anxiety, and the peculiar comfort of our shared peril.

Some of the worst jobs I've had were where I was a part of some of the best teams. Unrealistic deadlines or unsympathetic executives or unmeetable metrics can cause people to bond in ways that company retreats and pizza parties and all the trust falls in the universe can only envy.

In that moment, trudging through the uncertain dark, I felt the ghost of camaraderie more keenly than any spectral presence. The tunnel pressed in around us, but our back and forth pushed back at the suffocating gloom. There was a strange resilience in the way we kept moving, as if by walking together we could outpace both our nerves and the unseen things that might have watched from the shadows.

We continued on, senses tuned to the smallest sounds, the distant drip of water echoing like a metronome. Memories of failed projects and impossible targets flickered through my mind, the echoes of old challenges and unexpected alliances.

The corridor bent, angling sharply to the left as if the underground itself offered a compromise. We followed, the beam from my flashlight trembling over what looked like part of a rusting shopping cart and a heap of discarded missing person flyers, their colors bleached by time and moisture. Britney nudged a pile with her toe, revealing a faded sticker reading “Keep Out”, its warning long since ignored.

"Too late for that," she muttered, and I couldn't help but agree.

As the ceiling dipped, forcing us to hunch down, I caught a whiff of something floral beneath the pervasive damp, a hint of perfume among the dusty mold, or maybe just my imagination playing tricks. For all of its hazards, there was an odd intimacy to wandering lost with someone equally unwilling to turn back. If fear was the price of admission, then perhaps the payoff was this: discovery in every shared glance, every whispered joke that kept the darkness at bay.

We had no assurance there was an exit ahead, or that the ghosts in our wake were only memories and not something more tangible. But for now, we moved forward, two stubborn motes of light carving meaning from the underground's forgotten night.

A cracked opening to our right seemed to lead to a vertical ventilation shaft which could possibly lead to the street level. My flashlight couldn't reach the bottom and vanished into darkness towards the top as well.

Hysterically, I was reminded of the old text adventures my friends and I would trade on floppy disks approximately a million years earlier.

>view darkness

You can't do that right now

>examine darkness

You can't do that right now

>attack darkness

What is wrong with you?

>If I could answer that I wouldn't have to be so polite to my therapist and maybe she would still return my calls

Obviously, the underground was starting to take its toll on my sanity, and that wasn't a currency I was exactly flush with since I can remember.

The ventilation shaft was narrow enough that I could reach the other side, but the far wall was slick with some liquid I knew would result in my buying a new shirt in the near future.

One of the things they don't tell you about paranormal investigation or urban exploration when you take a course in either is that you need a bigger wardrobe budget.

I handed an end of Doug's rope to Brintney and tied the other across myself before wedging myself into the sticky awfulness of an unjustifiably optimistic ascent.

Chapter 19

Locking my joints against either side of the brick-lined passage I pulled myself upwards, more terrified of what is at the bottom of the shaft than what the fall might do to me. I had the distinct feeling that I wasn't the first person to attempt this climb, and that made it more horrible.

I also considered that Britney should be pulling herself up after me and while she was a slight person, it would still make my climb more difficult if I couldn't set myself to adjust to whatever weight she carried.

A ten-minute ride share to my real destination seemed like a choice Past Me should have opted for, but I can forgive that guy for not knowing what he was getting into.

Future Me is another person entirely, and I have very little consideration for his well-being. First of all, Future Me has never done a single thing to make my life any better and, most importantly, if he doesn't watch his step, I can ruin his whole life in an evening if I feel like it.

I'm watching you, Future Me. You are on thin ice.

What I had assumed was a vertical ventilation shaft trading bad subterranean air for fresh air from outside turned out to be something . . . It turned out to be something much worse.

The stains on all four walls were fouler than what I had guessed was just ancient condensation. It was organic and not industrial and if pressed I wasn't sure which option I would have preferred. Absolute immediate filth or possible cancer somewhere down the road? Again, Future Me should appreciate the good decisions I do manage to make.

My hands, slick with sweat and something far less pleasant, scrabbled against the bricks in search of a reliable hold. The smell in the shaft grew thicker, more oppressive, as if the ghosts of everything that had seeped down these walls were rising up to meet me. The rope between Britney and me tugged, the faintest vibration, and I stopped, heart skipping in staccato uncertainty. Was that just her adjusting her grip, or was something else, something below, testing the tension?

I didn't want to look down, but I did. The darkness below our feet was total, a pit so black it swallowed up the feeble glow from the flashlight. My imagination conjured too many shapes. Pale limbs, grinning mouths, the slick memory of other climbers who hadn't made it out. I shook my head. That was just the lack of oxygen or simple earned exhaustion talking. Or so I told myself.

Another few feet, and my elbow landed in a patch of dampness colder than the rest. I yanked my arm away, stifling a curse. The urge to scream for Britney to hurry was overwhelming, but I clung to silence, every muscle trembling from the effort not to panic.

Something tapped just above my left ear. A rivulet of water, or the tremulous legs of a spider, or maybe even the memory of hands reaching for a way out. I pressed on, forcing myself further up, desperate for the promise of fresh air, for any light that wasn't the murky phosphorescence of decay.

When I finally found a ridge, wide enough for the ball of my foot, I paused, listening for Britney's breath below, for anything at all that might suggest we weren't alone in this shaft. The walls, alive with secrets, said nothing. Only the rope between us, taut and trembling, reminded me that forward motion was the only option. I took a couple of shallow breaths and kept climbing.

Wooden struts eventually began to crisscross the tunnel, the wood damp and rotting but solid enough to use as a handhold if I didn't move suddenly.

Ominous creaks and pops echoed up and down the shaft and I quickly missed the earlier silence.

The shaft narrowed into a circle barely wide enough to get my shoulders through and then only one at a time before spilling me out of a stone bench onto a cobbled floor, the dusty remains of what may have once been straw completely failing to cushion my fall.

It seemed I had crawled up what passed for an ancient toilet and into a small room with only one other exit – a narrow door set with iron bars.

Trying not to think about it too much, I looped my end of the rope around one of the bars and began to pull Britney the rest of the way up.

It seemed like the coil of rope amassing at my feet should be more than fifty or even a hundred feet before Britney complained her way out of the narrow exit which shall not be named, but I'm not an expert in rope length estimating so I will keep my gripes generic.

It seemed like she hadn't climbed much at all. There. I said it.

The single other narrow exit from the room awaited, so I pulled out my lockpicks and reached through to access the lock side.

The mechanism seemed to be more rust than metal, too old and damp-clogged to pick but I leaned through the spare gaps between the bars and continued to try. I'll slam my face against the impossible until either surface gives up, and I have the rakishly crooked nose to prove it.

The scrape of shoes against the floor outside our tiny cell made me pull my arms back through the door and lean against the shadow-draped wall, gesturing for Britney to keep quiet, though she had been remarkably silent since we exited the waste shaft.

The steps came to a halt outside the door and more uncomfortable silence fell over us like a cloud.

Ghosts? Supernatural creatures? Some Celtic nightmare beasts come across the Atlantic to exact justified vengeance upon me? The cartels? Paparazzi?

Imagination is a curse.

"Miller?" the deep voice seemed to echo in the corridor outside our cell.

"Agent Jones?" I stepped into the sickly arrow of light leaking from outside.

"Nice phone," he nodded, "Your last one ended up in the parking lot of a truck stop in Phoenix."

"I'm not surprised," I sighed, "The same thing happened to three people I graduated high school with."

"And yet," Agent Smith said from somewhere out of sight, "we found you anyway."

"Did you think I was hiding?" I was genuinely curious, having decided anyone handing a device with a GPS feature to an IT security person was just collecting survey data on which ocean that might get tossed into. "I see too much weird shit to bother with the illusions we cling to that make us feel better."

"Who are you people?" Britney had finally found her YouTube presenter's voice.

"That's classified," two voices in lockstep carried through the still-locked door.

"They're with the Bureau of Rural Resource Management or something, Britney," I shrugged, feeling the unpleasant dampness of my shirt pull across my back in a way which threatened to make me gag.

"Actually," Agent Jones said, "We've been transferred."

"You can tell us where," I chuckled, "I don't care where you get your paychecks and Britney here is a YouTube personality, so no one is going to listen to either of us."

"Hey!" Britney objected, before lapsing back into silence. It's hard to argue against objective truth, I guess.

"Fine," Agent Smith announced, "We've been assigned to Project Nightwatch, part of the Office of Advanced Contingency Operations."

"Congratulations," I laughed, "I see they didn't upgrade your uniforms", gesturing at their Men In Black Halloween costumes.

"Why mess with the classics," Agent Jones smiled back at me in the dim light.

"Are you here to spring us?" I asked, hopefully.

"Yeah," Jones nodded, producing one of those multipurpose tools that firefighters use to ignore locked doors.

With a metallic squeal, the door yielded to the tool quickly. Or, more accurately, the wall crumbled around whatever locking mechanism had survived the decades down here in the dark and damp.

"You look like hell," Agent Smith told me as I stepped out of the cell, "and you smell even worse."

"Prison changes a man, Smith," I acknowledged.

"You were in there less than ten minutes," she scoffed.

"So," I nodded, "you admit that it's bad," checking to make sure Britney had stepped out after me, "Can you make sure Britney gets back to street level intact?"

"Nope," Jones shook his head, "We're going another way, and we need you to do what you do down here to quell some paranormal nightmare that's setting off sensors as far away as the Rockies."

"Sensors?" I asked, "What sensors?"

"That's classified," came the simultaneous response again. Is that an Illinois thing? Do people just say things at the same time? Does this have something to do with the Cubs? Or that weird pizza with the sauce on top?

"Put it to rest," Jones ordered, "Do whatever it is you do."

"And leave your phone on this time," Smith added, "You ass."

Chapter 20

Agents Jones and Smith exited the room downhill and we went the other way.

I tried not to think about why there would be a tiny room so far underground with an improvised toilet and a lock on the outside of the door.

I failed.

Holmes' infamous "murder castle" may have been demolished above ground decades before but down here in the dark some of his secrets could persist. As things tend to do, way down in the dark.

What had famously been a warren of secret passages and sound-proofed chambers above ground was also a tangle below the pavement, unmapped by city planners or historians. Unhoused people or travelers of all sorts could have become lost down here over the years and starved or worse, their stories forever untold.

"What is it you do?" Britney asked.

"I'm in IT security," I answered by reflex.

"No," she clarified, "I mean, probably. You're pasty enough. But they said for you to do what it is you do, and it didn't sound like fixing a printer."

"I'm going to tell you a secret, Britney," I leaned in, "But you have to promise to not credit me on whichever episode of your show where you investigate it, okay? I can't have anyone knowing I revealed this."

She nodded uncertainly.

"Sometimes," I looked both ways, "Sometimes the inkjet isn't out of cyan ink at all. It's possessed."

"You're a dick," she diagnosed.

"Sure," I smiled, "And you're a non-believer. And if we can get back to the street with you still being a non-believer, I will consider this excursion a success."

"Not a problem," Britney scoffed.

"I do hope you're right," I nodded.

I didn't think she was, but fingers crossed, right? Another adult unburdened with the knowledge that the world around them is weirder than they anticipate isn't a bad thing.

The Chicago underground isn't a place that coddles non-believers.

The first city cemetery outgrew its original home just before the great Chicago fire and was in the process of being relocated.

The stone markers had been moved already and replaced with wooden markers with the interred remains to follow when the fire swept across the grounds, incinerating all of the temporary markers.

It was impossible to locate and move the ten thousand graves lost in the fire, so it became Lincoln Park. A single mausoleum marks the location of the graveyard.

When they were building the zoo, a body was discovered and hastily reburied before a barn was built over the spot, so no one should be surprised that ghosts wander around.

There's a famous Lady in White who visits the Lion House and multiple spirits in Victorian dress fade in and out of view for employees and guests.

"You know, you could have just said you were in IT," she muttered, glancing back. "No need for bullshit ghost stories."

"But then how would you ever learn the importance of ritual printer maintenance?" I grinned. "If it starts printing only in Latin, I recommend running before calling the help desk."

Britney snorted, the sound echoing off the damp walls. The underground felt momentarily less heavy, less secretive.

We continued our hike into the dark, two skeptics navigating the threshold between the mundane and the inexplicable, each clutching their own version of reality a little tighter, just in case.

Chapter 21

The corridor narrowed, forcing us to walk single file as the old bricks pressed in, suffused with a chilly breath that settled on our skin like cobwebs. Overhead, the pipes groaned with the weight of generations. It was easy to imagine voices slipping through the mortar with the dust of history.

My flashlight beam caught a scrap of yellowed paper, curling in the corner where the wall met the floor. I bent to pick it up, but it crumbled under my touch, leaving only a wordless memory.

Around a bend, the tunnel unexpectedly opened into a circular chamber, its ceiling vaulted and adorned with the remnants of painted stars, fragments of some bygone attempt to mask the gloom with hope. We paused in the center, letting the silence gather around us, thick and unyielding. Somewhere above, the city continued its oblivious bustle, but down here, time stretched and folded in on itself.

Britney's voice was softer, "Do you ever wonder how many stories never make it out of places like this?"

"All the time," I answered, feeling a slow shiver that had nothing to do with the cold. "Maybe that's why the ghosts hang around. Someone has to stick around to remember."

We stood together for a moment listening for the barest hint of a footprint in the dust, or the brush of a spectral hem against ancient stone. And then, with a final reluctant glance at the painted stars, we pressed on, deeper into the labyrinth, our own story still unfinished.

The air, formerly smelling only of dust and stagnant water, began to take on the heavy smell of rotting garbage.

"As awful as it is, this is a good sign," I explained, "Old garbage eventually dries out and stops smelling like this, so someone has been dumping stuff from the surface down here recently."

"How is that in any way good?" Britney asked.

"Wherever the smell is coming from must be more convenient than surface disposal," I explained. The odor was getting stronger. "So, it must be open to the street or more likely an alley."

A narrow, crescent-shaped window hugged the floor of the next chamber, and the source of the garbage smell was unmistakable.

I knelt beside it and stuck the flashlight through the opening, revealing a pile of rotting produce piled up from the lower floor of the next room to within a few feet of the rounded window. Cabbages and carrots, wilted and rotting among discarded corn, tomatoes black with mold and unidentifiable fruits writhing with insects, all obviously discarded by some living person somewhat recently.

Pale, leafless tendrils announced unseen potatoes somewhere in the heap, growing upright like spider legs, searching for a source of light they would never reach.

The edge of my flashlight beam could just catch the bottom of a steel-lined elevator shaft on the opposite side of the room. And partially covered by that disgusting carpet of rotted produce.

I had just about decided it wasn't worth a potential exit to crawl through the wet mass of decay when the room around us, cast into darkness when I had pushed my flashlight through the gap, echoed with a wheezing giggle behind us.

"Oh, fuck every single thing about this," Britney announced before plunging headfirst into the pile of garbage below.

The burden of decision having been taken from me, I went legs first into the same pile, hastily pulling Britney out of the muck and hustling us towards the elevator.

The earthy smell of fungus assaulted my sinuses slightly less than the garbage-water smell of the cement room below, but it was a photo finish at best and tempered by my decision to buy new jeans before leaving Chicago and returning to the part of the world God still cared about.

I spent summers on the gulf coast, occasionally dragging a dip net through the surf because a crazy old lady my grandmother knew had heard the shrimp were running and they both probably thought I could use the exercise. It should be noted that in none of those attempts did I net a single shrimp.

But leg-wise, dragging myself against the tide was eerily similar to wading through decaying plant matter.

The old, hydraulic elevator's doors were half open, and I could see the smooth concrete floor of the car beyond them. I had no hope it was operational, but I didn't need for it to be.

We scrambled up the last clump of sodden turnips, the soles of our shoes squelching with every step, and arrived at the elevator's busted doors. The fluorescent light from my battered flashlight flickered across the interior, illuminating a scattering of rodent droppings and a single, cracked plastic badge. The air inside was cooler, laced with the metallic tang of machinery long past its prime. Another door, mostly shut, faced us from across the elevator car.

Britney, pants streaked with decomposing zucchini, pressed her face to the narrow gap over the doors, peering up the dim shaft as if willing the elevator to spring to life. "You think there's a panel somewhere?" she muttered, voice echoing off the concrete.

I wedged my shoulder between the doors, the corroded metal resisting for a moment, then yielding with a shriek. The sound stabbed the silence, multiplying our nerves. I forced a deep breath, my throat sticking with the memory of mold and filth. Beyond the threshold, the car's walls were scrawled with faded graffiti. There were dates and names and a crude sketch of a smiling cat defaced by a penknife.

Britney sidled in, her boots leaving muddy imprints, and crouched by a battered control panel. The buttons had been gouged out, their numbers erased by years of neglect. I doubted this elevator ever went to more than two destinations, down here and topside, and I didn't think it had even made that trip in years.

I stepped in after her and let the flashlight beam settle across the concrete, searching for any sign of motion. The stillness was almost reverent, a hush broken only by a distant, rhythmic drip. I weighed our options. We could climb up, risk the shaft, or try to force our way through the far door. Uncertainty hung heavily, but a new resolve seemed to have taken root among the rotting root vegetables. Desperation will do that to a person.

The security badge, splintered across the laminate, read only "CH––GO MUNI––" in faded block letters, the rest ground away by time and foot traffic. I kicked it into the gap beneath the doors anyway.

Britney listlessly and hopelessly pressed the "up" button while I pushed against the ceiling panels until I found the one that was a hatch to the roof of the car. A torrent of dust and worse things rained down on us as I finally managed to flip it open.

Propping a leg on the rusted bumper which kept cargo from slamming into the doors years before, I started the process of squeezing myself through the hatch and onto the roof. I cut my forearm on a filthy exposed bolt near the anchor point in the center of the shaft and was grateful to be up to date on my tetanus shots, though there was no telling what sub-tropical crotch fungus a guy could catch from wading through rotting vegetables so perhaps that was a wash.

I located the access ladder before reaching back through the hatch to help Britney out of the elevator and avoid the rusting bolt.

The access ladder went up a single floor and a quick hop through an opening roped off by yellow safety tape put us in the storage area for a grocery store. I could see stacks of packaged non-perishable inventory and the door to a large freezer, as well as the opening for a trash chute which explained where all the rotten vegetables had come from. In better days, the elevator would have carried a dumpster to that little room downstairs to catch all the garbage, but it looked like some of the current employees really didn't care about those details.

I didn't either as I spotted an exit door and led us through it.

Chapter 22

The grocery store was only lit by nighttime emergency lighting and the occasional illuminated freezer display, casting weird shadows across the walls and ceiling and reminding me that I hadn't eaten.

A quick walk through the produce section cured me of any lingering hunger. I doubted I'd be able to order a combo meal for some time due to my recent but justified potato phobia.

This market was a smaller store, stocked mostly with staples and tucked under the street level with a locked stairwell entrance and a single, separate elevator up to a parking garage and probably apartments overhead.

Somewhere in the gloom, a radio crackled out a static-laced snippet of top 40 hits, abruptly swallowed by a burst of feedback. The aisles were silent, except for the faint hum of compressors and the soft slap of our shoes against linoleum streaked with our muddy footprints. Britney trailed behind, her silhouette wavering between the shadow of a pyramid of canned beans and the glow of the freezer's blue light, arms hugging herself for warmth or comfort.

We navigated by instinct, dodging fallen boxes and the strange, glistening puddles that formed wherever condensation pooled. The air, still so pungent with the scent of spoiled produce and the attempts to cover that with chemical cleansers, made my eyes water.

A sudden clang reverberated from somewhere deeper in the store, a nervous reminder that we weren't alone. The building settling, a rat, or something less explainable, maybe. I didn't want to find out. We ducked behind a rack of plastic-wrapped tortillas as another sound echoed, a slow scrape that conjured images of janitors or night guards, though logic told me we were the only ones foolish enough to be wandering here at this hour.

The world outside was a distant rumor, and down here, under the low ceilings and flickering lights, all that mattered was finding a way out before someone, or something, came looking for us.

I hit the button to summon the elevator out of that space and the button obediently lit up. As it did, a giggle sounded from somewhere behind us.

I froze, my finger still pressed against the glowing button, heart thudding in my ears. Britney's eyes met mine across the narrow aisle, wide and shining with something between fear and disbelief. Another giggle, a little too sharp and a little too close, echoed down the corridor lined with breakfast cereals and paper towels.

The elevator doors shuddered, then slid open with a mechanical sigh. I motioned for Britney to move and she did, but our progress was impeded when we saw the bloody, decapitated corpse of a large rat in the middle of the elevator floor, so fresh I thought I saw a leg twitch.

"Nope," Britney announced, summing up my feelings on the matter.

Since we had probably triggered a motion sensor alarm the moment we stepped into the public area of the store, I didn't see a wealth of options for our escape.

We headed for the locked doors to the stairwell and, taking note of the two regular locks and the padlocked chain stringing the twin doors together I kept looking for options. It would take too long for me to pick all three locks.

In the end, I tossed a hot dog roller through the plexiglass door so we could crawl through and escape into the night, finally at street level again.

As we padded up the steps, I saw a tall, shadowy figure at the far end of an aisle, watching us as we scampered off into the night.

Chapter 23

The city never truly sleeps, and neither do its ghosts. Especially there, in the heart of Chicago's old neighborhoods where history clings to the crumbling brickwork and alleys echo with secrets. They say if you listen close enough, you can still hear the whispers of deals made in backrooms and footsteps that never quite fade away.

That night, it felt as if the past had settled over the streets like a heavy fog. We found ourselves drawn to the faded façade of an abandoned bodega, its windows long boarded up, its doors marked with symbols from another era, as if it had once been some speakeasy or illicit meeting house.

Ghost stories about Chicago have circulated for years; gangsters who refused to rest, debts left unpaid, and vendettas that bleed across generations.

I thought of the tiny Bachelors Grove Cemetery in the Everden Woods. Originally a settler's burial ground, the mob is rumored to have dumped bodies in the nearby flooded quarry during prohibition. Visitors report the traditional lady in white, phantom black hounds and even a house which appears on certain nights or under specific moon phases.

Residents of the buildings on either side of one of the parking lots for Lincoln Park report that snowy mornings are greeted with the outline of seven bodies in the snow, allegedly the victims of the infamous St. Valentine's Day Massacre which took place on the site. Ghostly machine gun fire and echoing sirens regularly pierce the urban gloom and dark shadows with wide-brimmed hats skulk around the space.

The ghost of Al Capone himself allegedly still frequents the shadowy back corner of his favorite club, the Green Mill Cocktail Lounge, while the ghostly bartender, rumored to be one of Capone's top assassins, still mixes drinks for his long-dead patrons from behind the bar.

Organized crime has left an indelible mark on Chicago that is immune to the passage of time.

Hymie Weiss attempted to avenge the killing of Dion O'Banion and was himself gunned down in front of the Holy Name Cathedral on October 11, 1926. The stray bullet holes were eventually patched except for one in the building's cornerstone which has resisted all efforts at repair for a century.

I could name half a dozen haunted Chicago hotels and given the history of the city there are many more, but I've had enough of haunted hotels to last a lifetime, so they can keep their secrets as far as I am concerned.

Any place where humans gather is going to accumulate tragedy over time, but many of the shadows of Chicago seem to dress themselves in dapper pinstripes.

Chapter 24

It was nearing midnight but a few blocks north of our escape from the underground was The Emerald Loop, a local Irish pub and the closest thing I have to a truly safe space these days.

While I had never been to that specific pub, it hardly matters. Some menus are more elevated than standard pub food, as The Emerald Loop was, but they follow the same rules of voluntary participation and dark and quiet corners that seem to become less and less ubiquitous as time moves on. If you don't go out of your way to cause a scene, an Irish pub is the perfect place to mind your business and not be bothered.

I ordered two Power's whiskeys and an order of fish and chips and went to work on my phone.

"Oh, did you want anything?" I looked up from my screen and asked Britney.

She chuffed out a quick laugh and went back to trying to reach her friends on her own phone. I barely heard the voicemail message start again over the ambient late-night bar noise before she hung up again in frustration.

The wait staff left us alone, but whether it was due to our focus on our phones or the garbage smell of our clothes I couldn't say. They did take and hold onto my debit card before bringing our food so you can infer from that what you will.

I texted my friend Natalie to ask, hypothetically, what a person's legal exposure would be if they were in an area restricted to the public and where they, again hypothetically, may have witnessed a murder. Or murders.

Even late at night, Natalie was quick to remind me that she was not that kind of lawyer, but she did suggest that I wear gloves and an N95 mask and a hoodie, which was a kindness, really. Normally she just suggests that I make better choices after I've already made the wrong ones.

I also texted Lydia, my other lawyer. Not that she could help in this situation either, I just needed to tell her about the Púca who was apparently hired to impersonate my dead friend to keep me off my game and eventually murder me. Lydia is a witch who specializes in contract disputes between us regular humans and the Fae. I don't know what that looks like day to day but if I texted any of that to literally any other person in my life they would assume I just stayed at that underground rave and took whatever stray pills I found on the floor. Which, if I'm going to be honest, sounds like a much better use of a Saturday night from where I was sitting.

At least until the fish and chips showed up, anyway. Fried fish is kind of a crap shoot. It's either light and flaky like a dream about the ocean or it's like you're a ghost being hit in the face with an oil-soaked five-pound brown paper bag of salt.

The Emerald Loop served the first kind and the whiskey helped either way, as whiskey does.

"Lloyd never answers but Doug should have by now," Britney announced, finally setting down her phone and picking up a piece of fish.

"Where did you guys go to access the underground?" I asked, "It's possible they surfaced there to call for help."

"I'm not a local either," she admitted, "but it was from the sub-basement of a Christian Science Reading Room."

"What?" I scoffed, "No way you guys went down from an active Christian Science Reading Room."

"No," Britney objected, "Really, we checked out the approved books, and then they let us wander down into the dark to meditate."

"I don't know that filming clickbait videos counts as meditation in many religions," I finished my whiskey and started looking around for someone to bring me another one before my ice melted.

"Okay," she smirked, "Maybe it's a bit of a grift for me. But you obviously make money off this paranormal bull-shit too, so don't act like you are morally superior because you've got a face more suited to podcasting than video."

"Ouch," I finally had another drink on the way, so my concern level was rapidly dropping, "but I don't actually make any money off any of this."

"Well," she sighed, "then you're obviously stupid. Geeks love this junk. Flail around with a camera in the dark and people will see what they want to see."

"What happens when you see what you don't want to see?"

"Are you still saying this crap is real?" she asked, dipping a sliver of fried potato into the tartar sauce, ignoring the ketchup in a way which managed to endear her to me, "Do you have a bridge to sell me?"

"I don't care if you believe," I matched her potato move, "A wise lady once told me that our beliefs have nothing to do with the reality of the world we live in. But what you don't believe in can still kill you, and I'd prefer to not be around if that happens."

"Aww," she laughed, "Aren't you sweet?"

"No," I asserted, gesturing at her phone, "My personal Yelp reviews definitely seem to avoid that word lately. Call your friends again, please."

She tried again but it went right to voicemail another time.

Lydia chose that moment to stop texting and just call me, so I answered and tried to figure out how to have a conversation in front of a person who didn't have any visibility into the kind of things we would be discussing.

Fortunately, Lydia did most of the talking, even if what she said was mostly unfortunate.

She explained a little bit about Púca physiology – Just enough to be really terrifying – and then went into a lengthy explanation of why the involvement of one of them didn't provide any real clue to which fairy court had it in for me.

"Our friend from New Orleans who liked your hair kept referring to them collectively as 'Themselves' as though that was a proper name," I explained.

"Ew," Lydia offered, "I don't like that. Grammatically, or in terms of general mood. I'll look into it from here."

I thanked her and ended the call.

"I can see their location," Britany announced, showing me her maps app, "It looks like they're a few blocks south, probably tucked into some dive bar, if I know them."

"Why do I suddenly like them more?" I wondered out loud, gesturing for the check and to reclaim my debit card.

We went back into the night, a light rain slowly darkening the concrete and muffling the sounds of the city around us as we traveled south.

Chapter 25

Chicago's South Side is famous for a lot of reasons. First of all, it's phenomenally ill-defined, with the borders contested by esteemed historians and rap artists going back pretty much forever, but however you draw the borders it is the largest geographical area of the city, followed by the North and West sides. I don't know if there is an official East Side of Chicago but if there is no one is singing about it or legislating around it.

For ghost hunters, Prairie Avenue is the place to be. Formerly known as Millionaire's Row, it boasts an array of haunted estates.

The Marshall Field Jr House is absolutely palatial and would be prime real estate today were it not for the dark feelings that wash over anyone who visits. Designed by Richard Morris Hunt, who also architected the Breakers and Biltmore estates for the Vanderbilts, it was the first house in Chicago to feature the extravagant luxuries of electricity and the associated lighting.

Famously, Field met Nannie Douglas Scott and was so taken with her that he leapt spontaneously on her train as it was carrying her back home to Ohio and proposed in front of a train car full of passengers who were joyous when she accepted.

The happy couple were married in Ironton, Ohio in 1863 in the social event of a season that was overshadowed by the blossoming Civil War, however much the guests may have been delighted.

Did they live happily ever after? No, this isn't that kind of book. Because our beliefs have no impact on our reality, remember?

Their loud screaming matches became famous on Prairie Avenue as insulation wasn't what it is today.

They divorced sometime in the 1890's and Nannie moved to France and, according to rumors, found her solace in the opium dens of Paris. She died in 1896 of an inflammation and is buried in the Field plot in Graceland Cemetery in Chicago.

Marshall Field the second remarried in England in a small ceremony with the neighbor who shared a fence in his backyard and, again according to rumor, died of pneumonia in a New York brothel in 1906.

Every time I am tempted to think my family is a little screwed up, I can look at literally any other family and feel better.

Today the building is the Institute of Design at the Illinois Institute of Technology.

Then there is the Keith House just down the block. It's an event space now because the limestone cladding and slate roof are as eternal as things get in the states.

Built by a former Presbyterian minister, Elbridge Gerry Keith, who wanted to live on Prairie Avenue near his two brothers, it is one of only seven surviving homes on the "sunny street that held the sifted view".

Six children were born in the house, I assume because in the 1800's people didn't know how to prevent that, but the house itself became a psychiatric hospital before it eventually fell into the hands of a publishing company and then ended up as an architectural bookstore. As fascinating as that sounds they could have probably made more money selling those upside-down pizzas the locals seem to accept as normal.

Elbridge was buried in Graceland Cemetery as well in 1905 and most of his estate passed to charitable purposes including the Moody Bible Institute, the Chicago Visiting Nurses' Association, the Chicago Old People's Home, Beloit College, the American Sunday School Union, and the Chicago Home for the Friendless.

Of course, specters make themselves known there and ghost tours are available whenever someone isn't getting married there or announcing a senatorial campaign.

Oh, but don't think that's the end of what Prairie Avenue can offer to the spookily inclined.

The Kimball House was built in a French style with turrets and enough architectural elements to classify it as "Châteauesque" on the national historical register in spite of that not being a word.

William Kimball himself made his fortune building pianos for our new country, so I can't fault him for much of anything. Music makes things better, even if it takes repetition and endless iterations to get through our thick western hemisphere skulls.

William Wallace Kimball's Chicago home is renowned for its carved stonework and impressive design. Since Evaline Kimball's death in 1921, there have been rumors of unexplained shaking of the north windows, with some attributing it to her ghost, but no scientific cause has been identified.

But all the rattling and skulking on the block pales in comparison to the activity attributed to the Glessner House at 1800 Prairie Avenue.

Henry Hobson Richardson completed the construction of it in 1887, the heavy, rough-cut facing stones calling back to Roman norms. It was his last project as he died three weeks after construction was finished.

I name the architect instead of the owner in this case because his ghost is generally the one most identified as walking the grounds and supervising the completed construction, rather than the residents of the house.

Sometimes what we love can trap us as securely as anything else can. It's not enough for me to advise against it, but love isn't something anyone comes out of unscathed.

Chapter 26

The rain picked up, spattering the pavement in dark circles. I was personally grateful for the illusion of getting somewhat clean as we hustled down the sidewalk, Britney checking her phone frequently to make sure we didn't pass up the location of her friends.

A whisper of black wings passed overhead and a flock of something passed in the dark. Pigeons or escaped parakeets or battlefield crows are identical in the dark to someone who skipped Nighttime Bird Identification 201 in their bullshit Biology degree, and I was more of a Classical Lit guy on account of the co-eds were hotter, but the goosebumps were substantial either way. Black wings are an ill omen, especially in Chicago where the Blackhawks are occupying the hockey franchise slot in the region and are, by all accounts, allergic to a winning season.

As we hurried along, the city's lights smeared across the slick asphalt, reflecting off puddles that collected at the curb. The sharp scent of ozone and burned petroleum mingled with the distant aroma of deep-dish pizza, and somewhere a siren wailed, echoing off the old stone facades. Chicago's ghosts might have been restless, but its living pulse beat on, unbothered by the legends swirling in the rain-soaked night.

Thunder rumbled somewhere in the distance, echoing off concrete and glass and sending a shiver through the street. The air had that charged feeling that always comes before a proper Midwestern downpour, thick with the scent of wet concrete and the heat of building electricity.

There is an energy in the area which can't be defined without description. One place I worked bought doughnuts from a local boutique.

Wait. I've never understood doughnut math, so this may be a tangent:

Remember the old Dunkin commercials where someone woke up in the dead of the night with the resigned "time to make the doughnuts" expression?

The whole idea of them was that someone was getting up to fry dough and coat it in sugar and (this is part that escapes me) sell the results of that effort with a hot coffee and you can leave with all of that for less than a couple of dollars.

Oh, if you're expecting me to go to that kind of effort, your printer is going to run out of ink on just the commas of that paycheck.

Our national doughnut infrastructure is woefully underpaid and I'm outside of the infrastructure, so I feel ill-equipped to do anything about it. But I am, as you should know by now, emotionally invested in breakfast food.

Sometimes, in moments like these, you realize it's not just the city's relentless bustle that keeps everyone moving. It's the subtle promise that, somewhere, a hot cup of coffee and a fresh doughnut might be waiting just out of the rain. The comfort of breakfast food, for all its humble trappings, can feel like a small rebellion against the night's uncertainty, anchoring you to a brief, sweet safe harbor amid the storm.

Britney pointed at an old building across the street which had been repurposed in an after-hours kind of place to grab a drink when the real bars closed. The crowd was mostly locals under a low ceiling covered in glittery rainbow banners.

I know you know exactly what that means but I will spell it out anyway: The drinks will be very strong and very cheap, but the music will be loud.

It was the kind of spot you might miss if you didn't know to look for it, tucked between a shuttered deli and a forgotten storefront with boarded-up windows. Somehow, the promise of a late-night refuge drew people in, especially on stormy nights, when laughter spilled onto the sidewalk and the warmth inside beckoned like a lighthouse. The whole scene felt suspended in the timeless hush that follows a thunderclap, inviting anyone nearby to join in and wait out the weather together with good company and strong spirits.

Lloyd and Doug weren't the couple performing *I've Got You Babe* on the karaoke stage, as much as I wanted them to be, so we took the long way through the crowd to seek them out. I'm sure that whatever the name of that bar was, it had its share of predators. Most bars do, but none of the ones in that place must have been interested in Britney and me because any kind of predator raises the tiny hairs on the back of my neck. As often as I poke around the restless dead, that feeling has sometimes been the only thing that kept me alive. I hated that feeling for that side effect as another performer took the stage for *Folsom Prison Blues.*

I got splashed with vodka and cranberry juice as someone yelled at someone named Steve to go to hell. He caught most of the drink on his Barbie-branded hockey jersey and stomped off to clean up somewhere in the back.

Completing the circuit, we settled in at the bar and ordered drinks while Britney fussed over her phone.

"It says they're right here," she shrugged, "but this is not their kind of place."

"Doug and Lloyd aren't into cheap drinks and anonymous crowds?" I took a deep drink of my whiskey, cold and filled up to the brim of a rocks glass, "Their loss, I guess."

"It stopped updating their location half an hour ago," she sipped at some fruit-forward rum drink in an enormous, stemmed glass.

"Maybe they're still underground," I posited, "Do you have a map of entrances?"

"Nah, Doug carried all that crap," but I could tell she was starting to really worry.

"Keep trying to call them," I suggested, "and I'll look around for one."

I tried to finish my drink in a single swallow but was unable to, so I asked Britney to keep an eye on it.

I didn't expect to return to the drink at all, since getting roofied and waking up missing a kidney wasn't on my bucket list, but I felt it was important to give her something to do.

The dark hallway at the back of the bar lead to a locked office and the restrooms, a side corridor blocked off by cases of warm beer and some unidentifiable sound and lighting equipment.

I opted to check the men's room before picking a lock or risking a scene in the lady's room.

The stickers advertising drunk driving attorneys were the least unsavory of the ample graffiti on the walls, sink and the two wooden stalls. Stained plywood took the place of the more appropriate tile on the back wall and pressing on it yielded a gap between two of the panels next to the stalls.

A piece of paper slid out and landed between my feet.

I picked it up, noticing the fresh blood along one edge above the spidery, bloody text, "This is your fault too, Lair, and now Doug and Lloyd will pay – Meghan"

The fresh blood on the concrete floor led me to open the closest stall, exposing Steve's headless corpse, neck ragged as though the head had been pulled off and not cut free, seated on the toilet. His severed head, spit-slick, was wedged behind the toilet paper holder under a glittering line of white cocaine.

I pulled the stall door closed and ran to grab Britney, shuffling her back towards the men's room and sliding the loose panel to the side, forcing her through and pulling it closed behind us before she could see the body and get us entangled with the authorities.

Her friends were in mortal danger and there was no time to waste.

Chapter 27

Along the shore of the lake was an area called "The Magic Hedge".

During the Cold War, it was a missile site and army base, situated there to protect Chicago and the Heartland against a Soviet attack.

The base eventually closed, but not without its own ghost story adding to the haunted landscape of the city.

Two soldiers serving at the camp were famously very good friends who would constantly argue with each other about any and everything.

One night they fought more loudly than they did most and one of them finally stormed off to the mess hall for a quick meal and to cool down.

Witnesses say there was a loud bang some time later and they rushed out to find the second soldier dead on the shore of the lake, with no visible wound or sign pointing to a cause of death at all.

His friend was distraught and ran off into the night. In spite of an exhaustive search, he was never seen again, and it is generally believed that he went into the icy lake and drowned.

Today the area is the Montrose Point Bird Sanctuary, and while visitors report that there is a stunning assortment of wildlife to be seen, on some nights they can see two figures animatedly arguing by the lake, whatever petty squabble they had in life spilling over into the liminal space beyond.

For years, it was an outdoor space where men would go when they were seeking the company of other men, but those days are long past.

Apart from the occasional fairy trickster assassin needing some ink, there are any number of bars and nightclubs in Chicago that are probably safer these days.

Chapter 28

I showed her the note by the light of another of my flashlights, and she asked the obvious question first.

"Who the fuck is Meghan?"

"Fair. Meghan is dead," I explained, "dead-dead, really."

"So why is she threatening my friends?"

"She's not," I stalled, dragging her along the pathway down into the dark again, "She has been replaced by a shapeshifter out of Irish mythology who will pretend to look like her for a price."

"For a price?" she stammered.

"I'm an IT security consultant," I objected, "People do a lot of unsavory things for a price."

She stopped mid-stride, halting our progress.

"I've seen some weird shit, Lawrence," Britney started, "but you can't expect me to believe there are Irish monsters roaming around Chicago, just casually eating people."

"What? You think they just eat that weird sauce-on-top pizza?"

"Stop being an asshole for just a minute," she asked, "Are we chasing a fairy tale into the dark?"

"I'm sorry, Britney," and I really, really was, "But that's the only place we can chase them."

"I don't believe you."

"That doesn't matter," I said, "but I wish it did, and I wish it more than you do."

She didn't answer, but we started moving downstairs anyway.

A rickety iron spiral staircase, orange with rust, headed down into the darkness.

The ancient metal creaked under our weight, each step sending echoes spiraling into the shadows below. The air grew colder as we descended, the faint tang of mildew and old machinery mixing with something else. Something sharp, metallic, and entirely out of place. Neither of us spoke, but I could feel the tension tighten in the darkness, the uncertainty hanging between us heavier than the steps we took.

My flashlight beam flickered across the damp brick walls, picking up faded graffiti and old stains that might have been water. . . or something worse entirely. Each step downward felt like we were leaving the world we knew behind, exchanging the comforting sounds of city life for the oppressive hush of whatever waited beneath. The silence pressed in, broken only by our breathing and the low, uneven groan of the staircase, as if the building itself was warning us to turn back while we still could.

At the bottom, the darkness felt almost solid, swallowing our light and muffling every sound. I could hear the distant drip of water echoing through the space. Every instinct screamed at me to go back, but duty and dumb stubbornness pushed us forward, step by hesitant step, into the unknown lurking beneath Chicago's streets.

Rough brick lined the walls and at least a century of construction debris littered the flagstone floor of what looked like an access chamber for the old transport tunnels. It was large enough to fit a horse and cart and carry goods, both legal and questionable, by torchlight without troubling with the traffic overhead. Or the watchful eyes of police or rival gangs, as needed.

A thin trail of blood led off into the dark tunnel, with drag marks through the dust on the floor.

Wordlessly, we followed after.

I tightened my grip on the flashlight, trying to pierce the gloom ahead as we approached a steel door, slightly ajar. Britney's voice was barely a whisper: "Ready?"

I pushed open the door to reveal a slaughter, blood pooled and splattered around a corpse shattered like a porcelain doll.

It had been Doug. I recognized his boots, sturdy without being expensive and rugged but showing so little wear on the soles I knew they were a costume.

A gaping wound like a crescent on his left side exposed part of a hip bone at the bottom and the sheared off tips of several ribs at the top of the arc. The exposed ends of intestines still leaked blood, but at a slow drip, very gradually widening the pool beneath him.

It was as if something enormous had just taken a bite out of Doug and discarded the rest of him like a popsicle stick here in the tunnels under Chicago.

Britney stood stone still, in shock as I muttered under my breath.

"We're going to need a bigger boat."

Chapter 29

The Púca is a shape-changer. This is different from a shapeshifter like my werewolf friends out west.

Werewolves and other (theoretical) shifters go from human form to something else. I mean, I guess there could be some cryptid monster out there who shifts between lobster and snapping turtle or something, but I don't see a lot of evolutionary advantages to that, so I haven't really given it a lot of thought. I'll explore it if I ever learn to draw and decide to publish a webcomic.

Shape-changers, on the other hand, can turn into whatever they want. They can be anyone you might pass on the street or take on the appearance of your dead friend. For example.

I don't know if taking on the form of an octopus would allow them to breathe water, but I also don't know if they need to breathe at all. Or if they could squirt defensive ink like a cephalopod or use discarded coconut shells as shelter.

The Discovery Channel has left a lot of very important information out about the way the natural world works. Or the supernatural world.

Whichever one it is that I live in.

Either way, manifesting a big toothy maw is well within their realm of abilities and would explain both this bite mark and poor headless Steve upstairs.

It was especially weird that I felt a kinship to this mercenary shape-changer, as that is entirely how I make my own living.

There's typically less murder in IT consulting but the core requirement for getting paid, in both cases, is in being exactly what is needed at exactly the right time.

There's no small part that involves getting your benefactors to pay for problems that you manage to create accidentally in the process of resolving other issues.

Allow me to go on a tangent about America's early history.

Philadelphia bought our Liberty Bell from White Chapel Foundry in London and when the bell arrived after its trip across the Atlantic and overland to Pennsylvania, it was broken. To this day, the White Chapel Foundry says this was user error and has refused to issue a refund.

But a plucky young blacksmith, trained in Malta, offered to fix the bell, for a nominal price.

So, John Pass and John Stow got the contract from the new government to reforge that bell. Neither Pass nor Stow had ever made a bell, and while it looked exactly like a bell, when it was struck it sounded like crap. Bell forging is different than blacksmithing, I guess.

Anyway, and the important part, is that Pass and Stow agreed to reforge the bell, adding other metals to the mix to improve the sound. In exchange for more money from the government.

The new metal made it famously crack pretty quickly but it sounded okay until it did.

And that's how Pass and Stow became the first IT consultants on the continent and kickstarted a whole industry of paying people for doing things just because you don't want to learn to do them yourself or be responsible for any kind of quality control.

If this sounds like an indictment, please know that I am forever grateful for these specific founding fathers for pioneering the grift which enables me to drink when I travel and leave that off my expense reports.

Anyways, it isn't the mercenary quality of the murders that bothers me. In this economy? We all need a side hustle. Who am I to judge?

It's the deaths, I guess. Would Steve have had his head bitten off if I hadn't been poking around in Fae realms accidentally? Judging from the drink thrown in his face, probably, eventually.

But Doug was a targeted kill, and he was never the guy who was going to be a target. That was me. I'm the one flailing around out of my weight class and only ever vaguely considering the consequences to the wider world around me.

When your focus is haunted houses, sometimes you ignore the yard. And the neighborhood quickly slips into somebody else's problem territory.

I had obviously failed at containing my activities to the haunted houses and, I suppose, eventually someone would come along to murder me about it.

Or, I guess, I could fix it through diplomacy but let me submit a handful of random Human Resources complaints about the things that I say in meetings which should magically dispel any ideas of that being a possibility.

I knew that we would have to face this Fae monster, this Púca, before we even got to the actual haunting which was hounding us. The giggling man, the mustachioed shadow in the dark. He didn't play by the same rules as a fairy mercenary. He was used to following his own rules, and we would need to figure those out if we had any hope of stopping him.

I paused for a moment, trying to piece together how we'd ended up in this mess. There's a certain inevitability when you're chasing shadows. One misstep and you're suddenly the center of a story you never meant to tell. Still, facing down the Púca felt like less of a choice and more of an obligation, as if the universe was nudging me toward a showdown that would test whether I'd finally learn from my reckless curiosity.

Spoiler alert: I will most certainly not.

I would try, maybe, but my effort would be tempered by my adherence to reality, so none of that makes any difference in this case.

I'd love to say that I had some great plan, some clever trick up my sleeve, but all I really had was stubbornness and a knack for getting in over my head. Each step forward felt like volunteering for another round of cosmic consequences, and yet, curiosity kept pushing me, even when common sense begged for mercy. This was never the story I meant to write, but maybe it was the one I was always chasing after.

Still, I couldn't shake the sense that every haunted house, every shadowy encounter, was part of a much larger tapestry, woven with threads I barely understood. There's a strange comfort in admitting you're in over your head; at least then, every tiny victory feels hard-won, and every failure is a new story to carry with you. Maybe that's what drew me to all of this in the first place: the hope that, somewhere in the mess, I'd find meaning, even if I had to keep stumbling through the darkness to get there.

Chapter 30

After a moment, we got moving again. I considered sending Britney back upstairs but figured she would just walk out of the wall and into what was probably an active crime scene by that time. She seemed resolved, anyway, determined to find Lloyd and make it back to the surface after maybe kicking a little Púca ass along the way. I knew it was equal parts admirable and stupid but saying someone makes bad choices isn't a brick I can really throw.

So, I kept an eye on the shadows around us and considered the city above our heads as we followed a thin trail in the dirt that we assumed was left by Lloyd or his supernatural captor.

Chicago is famously the home of a lot of weird stuff.

Remember the "Chicago Rat Hole" that went viral in 2024? A rat-shaped imprint in the sidewalk like the pavement had been carelessly installed over the corpse of a rat that lay quietly beside the street for over twenty years before being celebrated online, with people leaving flowers and coins and poetry at the site and documenting their pilgrimages on social media?

It turns out it probably wasn't a rat but one of the local squirrels that fell out of a tree into the wet cement and probably scampered away. Squirrels are active during the day when concrete is most likely to be poured and the measurements of the depression point more to squirrel than rat, but I'm not an expert on rodents, arboreal or otherwise. I try to not be too sad that it wasn't a rat – I prefer to just be happy that it happened.

The Chicago River, famously dyed green every St. Patrick's Day, actually flows backwards. Wanting to avoid sewage from the city flowing into Lake Michigan, which is the source of fresh water for the region, engineers in 1900 reversed the flow away from the lake. It also keeps the green dye out.

I've complained a lot about Chicago-style pizza, and it's delicious so maybe I should lay off.

No, it's just so doughy in the middle!

In 1930, Chicago gave us Twinkies which are still available and even battered and fried if you find yourself fine dining at a State Fair. They used to have banana cream filling but switched to vanilla during World War Two because there was a banana shortage and just didn't bother switching back. They do expire, so don't count on any still being fresh and delicious if that's all you've stocked your survivor bunker with.

Since people started flying in and out in 1955, what is now called O'Hare Airport has always been one of the busiest in the world. It has been expanded over the years, once with the city of Chicago spending $17 million to relocate all the residents of St Johannes cemetery with dignity and respect.

But they left Resthaven Cemetery, which is still an active cemetery today, at least as active as cemeteries get.

It's maintained by a small board of volunteers and new people are still buried there, but it has always been a small space, about an acre and a half, with the earliest markers dating back to before the Civil War.

Resthaven Cemetery sits south of the main terminal, tucked behind the FedEx hangars.

And, if you ever decide to visit Chicago and you're by some chance not having the best time, consider the passengers out for a sightseeing cruise on the river on August

8, 2004, when the tour bus for the Dave Matthews Band dumped an estimated 800 pounds of human waste from the Kinsey Street Bridge right on top of them.

Things may be bad, but in Chicago they can always be shittier.

Chapter 31

The sound of ragged breathing began to fade in and out somewhere in front of us.

Not particularly ghostly, as there was a certain humidity to it which spoke to the moisture of living mammalian lungs. That's not to say that it was particularly pleasant, just that the respiration was of the living, and I would like very much to make sure that it continued, no matter how uncomfortable it made me.

Anyone else ever miss masking? Personally, I developed a sneer at people who are being stupid, and I never bothered to stop when everyone stopped wearing masks. The pandemic was awful, but I taught myself to make candles so my apartment smells nice, and my masks were comedy gold.

The Púca isn't one of the Fae particularly associated with spreading plagues if that helps. Not that it means much. All fairies have their own domains of influence, but they aren't hard and fast rules, generally. Fae outside of the formal court structures are free to work for pay and the work they do ranges from mischievous to murderous.

It doesn't help that most of the documentation around who they are and what they do is maintained by counterculture types — witches and neo-druids and people who collect crystals for health reasons. I don't have a problem with any of these people, really, I just don't want them responsible for record keeping if there is literally any other option in the world.

But there isn't, so here is what we know:

Púcas are fairies. They typically act on their own and in their own interests.

They change shape, appearing at times as horses or large dogs or rabbits but also, if the need arises, they take on human form. This is always in the interest of blending in or fooling mortal humans.

They have been known to help people with their harvests or escort drunks (terrifyingly as a racing black steed) home from the pub or to even have long chats with people on park benches.

Their changes in form aren't tied to the cycle of the moon like with werewolves, so they can manifest a big toothy maw to eat a guy in a restroom and then squeeze through a keyhole to seek out their next meal. They aren't bad, unless they are paid to be, but contracts in the Fairy World are horrifically binding, so once one of the Fae accepts payment to do a thing, that thing is getting done or someone is dying. And often both things.

While most of the Celtic Ghost World, the realm of the Fae, is guided by strict rules and legal contracts (my friend Lydia tends to drink a little too much and rant about this) outside of the court is pretty much the Wild West for the Brothers Grimm set.

Most formal courts take advantage of this giant (meaning large, not actual giants, who may or may not be actual creatures) loophole to take care of things off the record. Or, as I would put it, to not make a whole thing about it.

No muss, no fuss, no one getting skinned and left in a bog for a thousand years.

I'm torn. As a fan of efficiency, I get it. On the other hand, as a current target for a Fae assassin, I'm less of a fan.

And the fact that I knew the hostage, however tangentially, made this feel even more personal than when my flight to Chicago was diverted to Minnesota and when the latte I got in that airport was obviously decaf.

The other thing about the Fae is that they are a petty folk. It's convenient to blame them for the natural calamities that just come with living, and it makes sense that people in the past would choose a scapegoat for their day-to-day drama, but that doesn't make in untrue.

Much like my complaints about Chicago pizza, things can be petty and dumb and true all at the same time.

It just can't cook right with that much dough, damn it. I don't think it's weird for someone to eat pizza with a fork, but you shouldn't have to is all.

We came across the remains of a raccoon, possibly washed down into the dark tunnel in a recent storm.

Every ecosystem has specific roles which must be filled in order for it to be considered healthy. Any lapse or deficit means the environment is out of balance or even suffering.

If you've got no predators, the prey animals breed out of control like tribbles on the Enterprise and if you've got no scavengers then things just kind of rot in place. Flies will colonize carrion almost immediately and bugs and rats are right behind. Even the apex predators will feed on found dead things, but this raccoon had been here long enough to suggest something was out of balance.

The local things which fed on flesh were avoiding this place, and I was afraid that they were smarter than Britney and I were.

The problem with feeding on other creatures is that there is always a bigger predator out there.

The wet sound of respiration became louder as we squeezed through a narrow bend in the brickwork.

Lloyd was there, bound in duct tape strapped across a rusted tangle of pipes. His eyes were wide and terrified, and his face ran with perspiration even in the chill of the tunnels. A filthy rag had been stuffed in his mouth but he managed somehow to whimper around it as Meghan stepped from the shadows behind him.

The grime of the underground seemed to have ignored her, and she hardly looked like she had been bothered by dragging two grown men around in the dark.

"Hey, Lair," she smiled, "Welcome to the party."

Chapter 32

"Don't call me that," I started pretty lamely, "You aren't as convincing as Meghan as you think you are."

"What did I get wrong?" she scoffed, "Hair too red? Legs too long?" She swished her floral skirt around her ankles.

"Nah, it's the eyes that are all wrong," I waved Britney to go around me as I circled to the right, keeping myself between her and the fairy tale monster in the dark, "Her predatory glares had a righteousness to them. You just look like you're waiting to get bored enough to kill something and get paid."

“I’m feeling pretty bored right now,” her voice was an eerie mirror of my dead friend. The sound was spot-on but the tone was off. Flat. Like a stereo recording played over a single speaker.

“The real Meghan found me entertaining,” I mocked an offended gasp with a flourish that let Britney inch closer to Lloyd.

“I’m sure she was humoring you,” she circled further, forcing me into a corner to keep her in front of me.

“Look,” I gestured broadly, Britney moved closer to Lloyd in the corner of my eye, “I don’t want to further bore you with some fight down here so close to some delicious authentic spots to grab a pile of pizza topside.”

“I’m not being paid to fight you,” her weird smile was too wide, like there were suddenly too many teeth to fit in a normal mouth, “I’m being paid to kill you.”

“What are they paying you?” I stalled, "I'll double it if you tell me who hired you and then just go home.”

“The price on your head is a pound of silver and a pound of gold,” her smile widened and, as I didn’t have a pound of either or any idea where a guy might get bulk precious metals in the middle of the night in Chicago, we both knew the negotiation portion of the evening was coming to a close.

A low moan from Lloyd drew her attention for a second and, while I still kind of wished I had carried a pound of gold and a pound of silver in my bag, what I did have was a spare five-pound brown paper bag of salt.

Salt doesn't have the same effect it does on the Fae that it does on ghosts. Salt is, as has been explained to me, Of The Earth, and it can unmoor restless spirits from the realm of the living. According to most legends, you don't get much more Of The Earth than fairies which are associated with nature and the cycle of the seasons.

But five pounds of salt, finally slightly damp from the humidity or my frequent trips through wet and disgusting places, is still five pounds.

Whoever thinks a pound of feathers and a pound of bricks weight the same obviously hasn't been hit in the face with both of them.

The Púca stumbled backwards, and I frantically looked through my bag for something else, anything at all useful in a fight with a shape-shifting Fae assassin.

When had I started collecting rocks and shiny trinkets like a deranged crow?

Most of my kit is assembled around ghosts and things from the spiritual side of the fence. Also, while I knew more about fairy tale monsters and their politics than I had a year earlier, I didn't know how to kill them. Other than maybe flinging a ghostly werewolf the size of a car at them when they aren't looking. Allegedly.

I had more salt and a tiny brass bell, some quartz and some sage and cedar, a few bundles of weird herbs Lydia gave me, as well as some witchy stuff I had no idea what to do with.

A hiss came from the Púca as she re-oriented on me.

I took note of Lloyd collapsing the floor – the tape had been the only thing holding him upright and it seemed like Britney had gotten him free of it.

One of the Púca's fingers elongated suddenly and stabbed into my shoulder even though we were still at least a dozen feet apart.

I fell to the concrete and clutched at the wound, weirdly grateful the weapon had been a finger and not a toe.

The Meghan-Monster began to circle, her grin widening again impossibly, forcing her ears back into her thick, crimson curls.

Her other hand shot forward, four fingers elongating into claws at least as long as I was tall, shredding my sleeve and doing no favors for the skin underneath, but not killing me. She was playing, like a cat with a wounded bird.

I'd have been insulted if I had the attention to give it while still trying to figure out how to not get eaten.

She laughed at me, a wheezing, guttural sound I'd expect from a pack-a-day smoker at the other end of a bar.

She crawled towards me, ignoring Lloyd and Britney altogether. I guess their role in this was finished for her.

I noticed that her knees suddenly bent the wrong way, and she seemed to have an extra elbow in the middle of her forearms, so while the resemblance to Meghan was definitely over it was still nice to have confirmation. Sure, I was about to be murdered down in a dark hole under a city famous for inedible pizza, but we have to take the victories where we can find them.

She skittered closer to me, still seeming to take her time for a humanoid with enough joints to move a lot more quickly. Stalking forward, her mouth opened to reveal multiple rows of razor-sharp, triangular teeth.

Her head shot forward like a snake striking on a suddenly long neck and I thrust my fist and arm into her expansive throat, fully expecting to lose the arm in the process.

The creature convulsed around my arm, tearing new holes in my flannel and ripping fresh lacerations into my forearm before collapsing to the concrete floor in a pile of ash.

I looked at the rusty iron nails from my bag that I had held between my fingers in shock before saying, "Huh, I guess that's how they work" and passing out.

Nicely played, Miller.

Chapter 33

On my earliest paranormal investigations, I didn't rely so much on gear. My pockets held my wallet, keys and phone and a container of mints.

I had an overnight bag I left in the car, but it didn't contain a bunch of spooky junk either, just hygiene products and a change of clothes in case I needed to stay overnight.

But a lot of my earliest investigations were unplanned anyway. Once a person starts to notice strange things, the strange things tend to notice you back. They get louder and more insistent the harder you try to ignore them, to rationalize them away, to comfort yourself with scientific reality instead of the less scientific one shrieking at you from the bloody skull over your shoulder in the bathroom mirror, for example.

During those first few encounters, I depended mostly on my instincts and a healthy dose of skepticism. The strange events rarely made sense in the moment, and I found myself improvising solutions with whatever was at hand. Sometimes, just talking into the empty air was enough to buy myself time, but most nights ended without answers. Only more questions and a nagging feeling that my reality was thinner than I'd thought.

I learned that was just the way of it, the default setting for a paranormal encounter. Ghosts and echoes of people aren't there to answer our questions. Most would prefer not to be there at all if they'd been given a choice.

Before I had any idea that I would ever bother with hunting ghosts, I was trying to graduate college on time. Having delayed the four PE credits I needed to graduate to my final semester, I was left with a courseload that included four dance classes.

I'll give you a moment to process that while I list them:

Ballroom, Ballet, Modern and Jazz/Tap.

I've never considered myself graceful, and neither did my poor instructors. There aren't enough left feet in the world to express how bad I was in each and every class, but

I figured as long as I showed up, I'd get the credit and get to leave at the end.

What I didn't notice in signing up for all of these was that the Jazz/Tap class included a final "exam" of a performance on the road at a fancy hotel up in the mountains for the overflow retiree crowd from Branson.

I arrived fashionably late for check-in to discover that the instructor hadn't booked enough rooms for my friend Jason and I and we would need to find accommodations elsewhere and make it to the 8am dress rehearsal the following morning, as if getting somewhere ready to do something at 8am was a skill I had developed by 22 and then conveniently lost for the rest of my adult life. We all have our strengths, and mine are never on display before noon on even my very best day.

As the front desk manager was explaining the sad news to our Jazz/Tap instructor, the young girl who was organizing the keys spoke up.

"We've got one room."

The manager turned to her with a dismissive wave and said, "No, we don't"

"The one up on Four," she offered.

"It's not for rent," he smiled, tightly.

"I saw it," she smiled back at him, "It hasn't been renovated but it looks clean enough for two college dancers."

I'll admit to having been a fairly jaded and world-weary twenty-two-year-old, but even if I wasn't, I'd have assumed the young lady was just hoping our gratitude would result in using our vast experience and well-earned maturity to purchase a six pack or two for her and her friends. And Jason could actually grow facial hair so he could probably even pull that off.

"There's no air conditioning in that one," the man warned us.

"No worries," I smiled lamely.

"Fourth floor," he grudgingly handed me a copper key, "Eighth door on the left."

The key was unmarked, but I could remember eight doors.

Jason and I decided to hit the town before dragging our bags (or in my case, cardboard box) upstairs.

My Texas and his Oklahoma driver's licenses got us into the first actual bars either of us had ever been in. Bars filled with neon and beer taps and overwhelming crowds of old people.

Over the years, I assume the crowds have youthened up into what I would today just consider "people", but I haven't been back to that part of Arkansas since (spoiler alert) I graduated.

We drank crappy beer that neither of us enjoyed and talked about school and the upcoming performance.

Jason wasn't nervous. Technically, while we were in the same group he was taking the fourth and final level of Jazz/Tap, having taken dance classes for his entire college career. He was actually being graded on his performance and was responsible for choreography for one of the routines. He had been kind to the clumsy people in the back row, out of kindness to me personally or out of concern for his grade. I didn't care which.

We called it a night early and headed back up the hill to the hotel.

It was a sprawling place, with dueling architectural styles and around eighty rooms and suites perched over an extensive spa and entertainment venue.

Back when it was new, it was a trendy place for the elite to spend their summers bathing in the allegedly restorative spring waters of the Ozarks. But that had been more than a century and a fire and several owners before my visit.

We walked past a nearly deserted hotel bar on the way in, our feet clacking on the vintage tile of the elevator lobby.

Wanting to put our stuff down before exploring, we took the glacially slow elevator to the fourth floor, and I counted out eight doors on the left.

There was no number, partially explaining the unmarked key.

The room was tiny, with two twin beds wedged in the middle with only enough room for a person to walk sideways between them. The furniture was solid, but old, the mirror clouded with age or possibly stained by smoke.

We quickly set down our things and tried not to flee into the hall, both overtaken by unease by the old place, the subtle signs of age, the more obvious appearance of disuse.

I tried to laugh it off, but the echo lingered oddly against the aged wallpaper, making me wonder just how many stories these walls had soaked in over the years. Jason shrugged, attempted to paint on a reassuring smile, and suggested we go see what the hotel looked like at night. I agreed, if only to escape the oppressive closeness of that tiny room for a while longer.

The bar downstairs had a single patron, a man sitting by the window. He didn't look up as we entered, and we didn't wait around for a bartender to show off our IDs again.

We found the old stage where we would be performing in what had once been a ballroom, now filled with banquet chairs in anticipation of the tourists visiting to see us dance after they'd hit the buffet.

The hallways were dark, lit only with emergency lighting as it slipped past the polite time of the evening and we passed the old spa rooms and spring-fed pools. Past a locked room with a metal table and what looked like a walk-in freezer in a dark corner.

We finally gathered the nerve to try to sleep in the tiny room we had been given, and I can recall the sound of what I assumed was housekeeping pushing a rusty cart down the corridor outside as I drifted off.

I woke up in the dead of night to find the room cold enough that my breath fogged the air and to see a tall, angular figure standing at the foot of the beds, directly in front of the narrow channel between them. It didn't move, but it watched us both as I tried and failed to move, or warn Jason, or even just whimper quietly.

I must have fallen asleep again, because the bright light of morning hit my face from the gap in the curtains and Jason was gone, along with his things.

I quickly showered and tossed my things into the cardboard box before heading downstairs for breakfast.

Years later, I learned that the hotel and spa hadn't always been a hotel and spa. It started as one, but the popularity quickly faded until it closed.

It reopened as a dormitory but was too expensive to use for student housing and closed again.

In the 1930's, it opened again as a quack cancer hospital. The corpses were wheeled out of the building on a rusty metal gurney after 11pm to the basement room with the freezer so the other patients could be told people were just getting better and then going home.

By the time of our visit, it was a hotel again. No longer chasing the original opulence, but an icon overlooking the valley beneath it.

I had just convinced myself that it had been a nightmare and that I was crazy to still be shaken by the overnight visitor when I found Jason and set my box next to his suitcase.

"I'm sorry I left," he said, "But that tall guy freaked me out and I couldn't stay in that room."

Chapter 34

Over the course of a very long career, I have been knocked unconscious a problematic number of times. Each one is different, a unique snowflake of catastrophe which paints the occasion into a rainbow of Traumatic Brain Injury which the NCAA would gleefully defend as "just a part of my process".

In this case, I was happy to wake up to see Lloyd and Britany hovering over me, concerned that I might not wake up.

New ghost hunters are adorable like that. The fact is, none of us come out of it without lasting damage. That's the way paranormal investigation most crosses paths with just being alive.

Once you realize everything damages everyone, your association with that same everyone changes. Being suddenly brothers in arms with the rest of humanity colors your interactions with them.

I'm not great at a lot of things, but regaining consciousness is a skill set that I can rely on. And if I ever can't, that is the very definition of someone else's problem.

"That bitch ate Doug," Lloyd complained, somewhat uselessly. I guess I did learn that Lloyd had been conscious for at least part of his abduction.

"She's not eating anyone else," Britney kicked at a pile of dust, "But she may still trigger allergies."

I busied myself wrapping my savaged arm in the only reasonably clean pair of socks in my bag.

"We need to find another way out of here," I explained, not really looking at either of them while I worked. Blood quickly welled up through the cotton and spandex blend, "The way we came in has too many corpses to remain hidden and we all look like shit."

"Hey!" Britney objected, "I'm not camera ready but you guys look like you got dragged down here through a mountain of wet angry cats."

"Wait," Lloyd interrupted, "Bodies? Like plural?"

"It's been a long night, Lloyd," I stood up, feeling the drying blood pull at my flannel and wondering if I had any chance of making my appointment and, more importantly, my flight home. But I guess there were probably more pressing issues.

"I'm sorry about Doug," I said, and I meant it, "I recommend you guys head to a police station and report him missing as soon as possible. If they haven't found him yet, they will before long."

"What do we tell the cops?" Lloyd looked ready to panic all over again. I didn't think his heart was up for that.

"Tell them your friend is missing," I explained, "No details, you just got separated in the dark. It's not like either of you took a giant bite out of him."

I realized I was being unkind. This wasn't their fault. I mean, other than them choosing to wander around a haunted place all unprepared in the dark and all.

"I'll handle it, Lloyd," Britney tried to assure him, "You just go to the hotel and I'll deal with everything."

He nodded numbly and swayed a little. She was right. He couldn't manage an interview anytime soon.

"It's not easy," I admitted, "I've lost someone on an investigation before. I can't tell you it gets better, but you can survive it if you want to."

"I'm not sure I want to," Lloyd murmured, "Doug was my best friend."

"Doug would want you to live," Britney suggested, and I stepped back from the conversation as consoling people isn't a gift I was blessed with.

Lloyd sniffed loudly but nodded. I noticed his breath fog the air before I felt the cold descend on the brick chamber.

A giggle cut through the air a half second before a mustached man in an old tweed suit appeared over Lloyd's shoulder.

I ran forward, intending to push Lloyd out of the way and deal with a ghost, something I was actually prepared to do, but I wasn't fast enough.

The man brushed the back of his hand against Lloyd's cheek. There was a small flash of light and Lloyd collapsed to the floor. His eyes went glassy before he was halfway down.

"No!" I yelled, "We were safe! We were done!"

The man reached forward, still smiling, and laid his hand on my chest next.

Chapter 35

There was a small flash of light again – A flicker, really. But I met his rheumy gaze as his eyes grew wide and I didn't fall. I felt like I should.

I had seen this ghost knock the soul or whatever out of at least two people but he slapped at my chest again like when I told that theatre kid in college that Phantom of the Opera was overrated.

In my defense, I'd been drunk. That is my defense a problematic amount, probably.

The man in tweed sneered behind his mustache and faded away. I was grateful he didn't giggle, at least.

"What the fuck was that?" Britney shrieked, too close to my ear to be considered polite.

"I think that was H H Holmes," I shrugged, "or whatever is left of him anyway."

She knelt on the damp concrete and checked for a pulse, but I think we both knew Lloyd was dead. It didn't look like he had felt anything. Whatever had made him alive was just gone somehow at a touch from this ghost.

"You have to make sure that guy doesn't touch you," I suggested, "I don't think I've encountered a ghost this dangerous, and certainly not one who seemed to take everything so personally."

"Holmes was a narcissist," she looked like she was reading from an invisible Wikipedia page in front of her, "Killing people was a bonus for him, he just wanted to win at everything and that was the simplest way to keep score for him."

"So you guys did research this guy before crawling around under his house?"

"My commentary keeps me from just being a pleasant t-shirt on YouTube, Lawrence," she didn't sound as offended as I thought she could, "I read up on the guy on the flight over."

"I've never seen your show," I defended myself, "I have no opinion on your wardrobe choices."

"His favorite victims are women but he liked just killing people more than he did discriminating," she shivered.

“I can appreciate an equal opportunity murder ghost.”

“He tortured people down here in the dark,” her eyes were wide and terrified, “This was more than some sick hobby. He felt killing was a compulsion and was eager to give into it. Almost proud.”

“A predator,” I nodded, “and one willing to keep up the work even after he died.”

“Oh, death fascinated him,” she nodded, “He felt his work was in service of death. He would never consider it an obstacle."

"After a while, I guess if anything it seemed more like a welcome companion than some abstract concept."

"That’s it exactly,” she looked at me, “He surrounded himself in death on purpose, he fed it, almost worshipped it.”

“That’s dark.”

“He died thinking death owed him something,” she rubbed at her arms for warmth, “He thought he was immune. More than anything, his own death probably surprised him.”

There’s a certain human instinct that tells us we are immortal. It lets us take risks, step out of the routines that make us comfortable. A little assumed bullet-proofing is part of how we change and grow as people.

But it's perilously easy for that little illusion to become a problem. In moderation, most things are fine. It's excess that kills us, and it sneaks up on a person.

"He knows we're down here," she glanced around, "He won't give up until we're dead or far away."

"I think we should opt for the second choice," I said, heading for the exit.

A slight figure in a tight black dress appeared in the doorway back to the tunnel we had come through.

"We all make choices," she smiled, "and yours has paid off for you."

She gestured to where her pendant rested under my shirt.

"Oh," I started, "Hey, The Morrigan."

"It worked, didn't it," she didn't ask.

"Yes," I smiled, "Thank you."

She stopped smiling.

"Never say 'thank you' in this world," she shook her head, as though she was admonishing a child, "It implies a debt is owed, and a payment is to be collected."

I tilted my head like a confused dog. "Sorry about that," I shook my head.

"That's even worse," she reached forward and plucked my left eyeball out with her long fingernails.

Britney later informed me that she tilted her head back and swallowed the eye like a crow, but I was already on the ground, clutching my face and writhing around.

"Now," The Morrigan said, "We are even."

Chapter 36

I'm not ashamed to say it took a minute for me to get moving again. I wrapped a strap of flannel around my head mostly because the eyelid kept blinking over nothing and making a popping sound that was almost as bad as the pain. Packing it closed with another wad of cloth at last stopped that and helped to slow the steady drip of blood down my face.

I collect injuries in this line of work like they are Magic the Gathering cards, but if I were somehow forced to pick the worst, losing an eye would be top of the list.

I felt my head pull constantly to the left, trying to fill in my new blind spot as I frantically searched for a new exit to the surface. I instinctively held my arms out in front of myself, uncertain of my depth perception in what was already an environment bordering on pitch black. My left cheek began to pull as some fluid, probably blood, dried on the skin.

My mother's medical advice echoed in my head as I stumbled along in the dark. "Don't pick at it."

Wasn't one of the many weird things we learned about ourselves during the pandemic just how much we love touching our own faces? I had no idea before the CDC said that it was a bad idea but it seemed at the time to be one of my very favorite things.

The urge to cover my makeshift flannel bandage was quickly overwhelming and I stopped, knowing that continuing to move forward while distracted was the quickest way for me to get Britney and I killed. Or worse, depending on what it actually was that the ghost of Holmes could do to a living victim.

The Morrigan seemed to think that he could absorb the soul of whoever he touched, but I'm still not sure I believe that is possible. Sure, her pendant had probably done something, not anything worth an eyeball in my opinion, but I wasn't convinced this was strictly soul-related or anything.

I sat against a damp stone wall and waited for my head to stop spinning while Britney paced across the tiny chamber I had stopped us in.

Organizing my thoughts is part of the process, so I started to put things into piles based on my ability to do anything about them. Hurling myself against obstacles I wasn't able to change was wasted time and energy, so I set aside another place in my brain for that, the very bottom of my to-do list.

I needed to check in with Jones and Smith. First to see if they had access to some kind of secret government medical care and also to see if taking out the Púca had taken care of their action item for me.

Lydia was probably waiting for a call letting her know that I was alive. That could wait as the jury was still out on that one.

Both of those required my phone, which had no signal and low battery. Bottom of the pile.

Longer term, the Fae had just taken a swing at me and killed a bystander. They had gotten another one killed by dragging him beneath the famous Chicago Murder House. Maybe I needed to go on the offense, but who was I kidding? I needed to hide, to get off the Fairy radar for a while. I wondered how being an immortal fairy tale monster would alter someone's ability to hold a grudge.

I had promised a restaurant manager he would be ghost-free before his brunch rush, and while that was lower priority, it was still something I considered important. And doable if I could get topside in time.

Coming back to Chicago anytime soon was off my list entirely, so if it was getting done, it was getting done before dawn which was just a few hours away.

Top of the list kept swimming into focus as I tried to compartmentalize my task list and the fresh giant hole in my face.

I had to get Britney to the surface and out of danger, so at least a few blocks away from Murder House central.

“Let’s get moving,” I said as I staggered to my feet.

“Are you sure?” Britney asked, “You don’t look great. I can get back to the surface and send help.”

“No way,” I tried to stand up straight, but my legs didn’t cooperate and my shoulder still hurt from the submarine accident, “We can’t split up now. Holmes is still out there and he has an agenda. I can’t know that you’ve made it and you won’t know that I’m still alive if you do.”

“Fine,” she agreed. "But we take the first staircase we find, and we follow it to the end, okay?”

I nodded, noticing more drying blood had made my neck sticky. I added putting wet wipes in my kit for future excursions to my list of things to do. It went somewhere in the middle, for the record.

The first staircase we found spiraled down further into the dark of the underground.

So did we.

Chapter 37

I know, we needed to go up, so going down seems counter intuitive, but the way these tunnels layer on top of each other, it's even odds that a lower level can have a more direct route back up than a gradual ascent might. And, as most places we had been had been varying degrees of horrible, the idea of a new place to explore had some appeal just based on it being new to us.

Not that where we emerged fit any definition of new other than geologically.

Worm-eaten wood lined the walls where it hadn't rotted away completely, but at some point, this area had been higher up – if not above ground completely.

Plenty of Old Chicago had been built over as time passed, with whole blocks receding into the earth as heavier stone building were placed on top of them. The streets above are still known to sink as the decades roll past, and developers have been known to just pave over and rebuild to avoid costly archaeological surveys pushing back their construction dates which sometimes results in whole structures gradually being pushed down into the earth under generations of taller and taller and heavier and heaver buildings.

This space was abandoned easily a century before and probably closer to a century and a half. It looked residential rather than industrial, so at some point it could have been part of one of the large houses by the lake built for the earlier, wealthy residents of the city. It had stood up over the decades because it had been constructed before "balloon framing" took off in the area as a way to cheaply and quickly put up new buildings. That style went out of fashion in the area when it fueled the Great Fire, but this house, build with post-and-beam construction, had survived the fire before being abandoned and eventually paved over.

Even the most solid wood construction has a sell-by date, so it wasn't a safe place anymore, but it possibly led to an exit we could use.

The space smelled like mildew and dust and the weight of history which has been forgotten but still carries meaning – Just possibly not for the living anymore.

Another flashlight gave up on this adventure so I pulled out one of only two I thought reasonably might still have some charge remaining. If it came down to it, I had a few white emergency candles in my bag but we would need to be somehow even more desperate before I relied on those for navigation.

I swung the light to the left a little more aggressive than strictly necessary, but without an eye on that side the shadows just seemed particularly dark to me. Being a cyclops was going to take some getting used to.

The skeletons of what had once been nice furniture sat in the corners, nothing left but wood and some horsehair stuffing, everything else rotted to dust or carried off by vermin long before.

The light glinted off a pile of glass orbs covered in spatters of melted wax. Most of the balls were cracked and empty but a few still sloshed with liquid when I toed them with my boot.

This place must have been older than it looked, I figured as I carefully placed the full ones in my bag, making sure they couldn't touch each other and clink together. They were sealed with ancient shrunken corks and some kind of plaster. I was aiming for being as silent as possible when a wheezing, masculine giggle in the dark behind us reminded me it hardly mattered.

We moved deeper into the old house, floorboards barely creaking as they pressed into the cold mud beneath them. The architecture of the space began to reveal itself to us in the stabbing light of the flashlight.

We had arrived through the crumbled wall of a sitting room, passed a foyer and into a kitchen marked with the piles of rust which had been fixtures or possibly pots and pans.

The remains of what today would probably be a full-sized bed marked a bedroom, but it had been chewed into sawdust by something years prior. Rusted hinges and warped planks of wood stood in place of what had possibly been a wardrobe, the clothes inside long gone.

A battered hardwood staircase, the railing torn away, ascended into more darkness and we wasted no time in trying to gain some elevation, our steps loud as the wood groaned under us.

The ghost of America's first documented serial killer knew where we were anyway, and he didn't care at all that we were aware of it.

Chapter 38

One of my favorite reasons that Chicago is a terrible place is also one of the very many reasons that I hate Florida.

As someone who has an adult-onset apple allergy, no matter how much I'd like a cider, especially mulled when the air gets a touch of a chill, that is forever a spectator sport for me.

Apples make my throat itch. Malt makes it difficult to breathe. Fresh-cut grass can send me into a coma.

Not to brag, but my immune system is willing to go scorched earth for a ton of random nonsense.

The tradeoff is that I'm not allergic to poison oak or poison ivy. Put that stuff in a salad and I'll drown it in ranch and pick around the cucumbers which taste like swimming pool water to me.

Not going to lie – Dating is difficult for me. I can seriously go right to ordering spaghetti on a first date because getting tomato sauce all over myself has approximately zero chance of making the top forty reasons to decline date number two.

Oh, but the same Chicago World's Fair that H H Holmes used to prey on out of town guests for his Murder Castle, also has a well-documented cider issue.

Florida was one of the states that had a pavilion at that fair, and their big seller was an orange cider. It was sweet and fizzy and had fresh orange juice in it, because at the time Florida didn't have much else going for it other than being a suitable climate for growing citrus fruits. Modern day Florida has other things to brag about.

I can't think of any of them right now but that doesn't matter.

Anyway, this non-alcoholic orange cider was reportedly delicious and so popular that other pavilions at the state fair started producing their own.

The problem was none of those used actual orange juice. They used water from Lake Michigan and red and yellow food coloring and molasses, with varies recipes producing results which were inconsistent at best. One of the predominant jokes at the time was a fair vendor showing up at the local grocery and asking for dye and water and terming it an emergency because they were out of cider.

The marketing hit that the potential orange cider industry took was enough to relegate the state to punchline status for over a century. So far.

As a person with an apple allergy, I'm more than a little pissed about this turn of events, because in any other reality I could drink some booze made out of a fruit that doesn't make my throat itch, But here we are, in our apple-centric cider economy with me restricted to drinking non-fizzy, unfruited whiskey for refreshment no matter what time of year it is.

Actually, I'm not measurably upset about that at all.

This early World's Fair was designed to steer us as a species towards our best possible selves, the arts and culture as well as our collective technological advances on display so that we have no excuse to move backwards.

I mean, a lot of the time we did it anyway, but at least we didn't have an excuse. We have to take the victories where we find them, even if they involve some weird Floridian cider.

Chapter 39

The giggling kept pace with us as we moved through the surviving upstairs of what had once been a very nice house.

There were curtain rings on a rusted rod in front of an avalanche of earth from a shattered window. I wondered what the view might have been. Possibly the lake, as someone watched the waves and waited for a loved one to return on them.

Or, as I was more than a little disoriented, maybe it had been a view of the bustling streets of early Chicago, before the Great Fire and the Cubs got cursed and this was the leaping off point for expeditions to the only vaguely explored Out West.

I guess technically it might have been the view of an alley or of the side of a building next door, but those are less romantic so I'm going to assume some view of value was lost as this home sank.

At least I have the decency to admit when my narratives are bullshit, okay?

The giggles continued to bounce at us from every flat surface. I wasn't timing them, but I still knew they were arriving closer and closer together. I've spent more than the average amount of time in haunted places against the very sound advice of well-meaning and sober advisors. This hasn't impacted my behavior at all, really, but it has given me an innate sense of when that ignored advice will seem prescient and things are about to go sideways.

We looked somewhat frantically for an exit in the decaying ruins of this lakeside home, trying to stay together while we dashed from room to room. We noted empty bookshelves and a large, glass wall hanging that may have once held a map before the beetles found it.

Leather stretched like mummy skin across the framework of a desk chair in the corner, circles carved into the thick dust underneath it as if it had been regularly moved over the past century even though the house had been empty of the living.

Another giggle crept up my spine and I almost longed for a chance to confront that thing in the dark, just to make it stop. I'd could count wiping the awful smile from beneath his mustache as a victory, though I knew that paying for it with human souls was too steep a price for me.

"There!" Britney yelled, pointing off to the left.

I had to turn to see a tweed-clad sleeve vanish into a wall.

I sighed, leading into a session of trying to regulate my breathing and reminding myself that my field of view was half of what I was used to.

Objectively, it was better than having my soul eaten by some psychopathic dead guy I guess, but it hurt and I was still adjusting to the loss in capabilities.

I don't know what IT security consulting looks like with an eyepatch, but it was pretty far from my mind as I was still struggling with what everything looked like from behind one.

I felt a fresh trickle of blood escape my hastily constructed flannel cocoon and run down my cheek. I didn't think I would be bleeding out from the wound, but common sense told me the longer it took me to get to a hospital the worse the recovery would be.

The thought of some emergency room technician having to clean out my left eye socket before treating the injury was enough to make my stomach drop into my lap, so I did whatever I could to avoid thinking about it.

I'll never say my process is good, but I will instead stress that it is just well-established.

From the corner of my eye (singular), I saw another flash of tweed and I staggered to put myself between it and Britney.

"I can take care of myself, blinky," Britney objected, and in spite of the barb I had some respect for her wanting to take care of herself.

I guess in some way, Britney and I were both working in the same emotional space.

I was missing a great part of my sense of awareness, but she was coming to terms with the fact that the paranormal, which she had been using to keep a roof over her head, was actually a real consideration worthy of the attention that she was paid for it.

Our comfort zones are a survival mechanism as much as anything else is. We learn what works faster than we learn anything else and there is an evolutionary reason for that. It keeps is alive and it lets us make terrible decisions later.

If there is a divine power, I dare you to try to convince me that they don't have a sense of humor.

The scent of wool and damp and rot swirled around us as we instinctively pivoted back-to-back behind one another and waited to see what the next challenge would be.

I was heartened that Britney would accept my help and was willing to trust that hers wouldn't be dependent on likes and subscribes.

At some point in a paranormal investigation, you just stop asking what "real" is.

Chapter 40

With my limited field of view, it was nearly impossible to keep myself between Britney and whatever tweed monster was about to ignore the laws of physics and appear out of some random wall and ruin our night.

The giggling got louder and louder as we circled as I dug around my bag for something to make a difference.

The spectral stuff I can handle, generally. It's not like it's fun, exactly, but I've spent years dealing with variations of this exact nonsense.

Sure, this ghost was deadlier and probably more sadistic than most I had tangled with, but the rules are always the same.

Sage for purification and Palo Santo wood (sustainably sourced) as a deterrent. And a big fat bag of table salt to remind the guy that he's only tethered to this realm by his own vague idea that he should be.

I just needed him to show himself to let me get to work.

A phantom wind began to pick up bits of detritus from the area around us – splintered wood and dust, mildewed papers and scraps of ancient wallpaper. Probably worse things, but not anything I would waste time considering.

One of the downsides of hunting ghosts for a long time is the tendency to get complacent. You've seen one specter and you've seen them all, right?

Typically, they flit around the shadows, lurk in dark corners, hover over the beds of the peacefully sleeping. Ninety-nine times out of a hundred, you know what they are going to do, because sometimes the haunting classics are the classics for a reason.

So when the ghost of H H Holmes hurtled out of the wall and bum-rushed us, I will admit that I was taken aback.

This mustached, tweed-draped monster was apparently done with lurking around and giggling from the shadows, and with sunrise on the way he was possibly feeling the timer even more acutely than I was.

I stepped instinctively to the right, the space I could see, and tried to keep him from even brushing against Britney. I was protected, but she wasn't.

He passed through me, freezing the air in my lungs and highlighting the array of injuries I was hosting.

Every ache and pain I carried answered his ghostly call to action. My face, my shoulder, my ribs. When had I hurt my hip? Was this what getting old felt like or would I be better off with a safer hobby like knitting or pickle ball?

Objectively, probably, but I rang my little brass bell anyway.

I don't know what it is about the sound of a metal bell, but most ghosts hate it.

Maybe it is something about the sound of church bells or possibly it's just an issue with the resonance of the sound itself, but most of the time the sound of a bell will send a ghost running for a little while. All you want with that is a smidge of delay so that you can deploy the big guns of paranormal adjudication.

In this case, the sound of the bell didn't seem to do much. It's possible H H Holmes was just not religious enough in life for the sound of a bell to matter to him, or possibly his ghost was just too powerful and determined to be put off by the normal means of mitigation.

That's okay, I thought, because I've grown as a paranormal investigator and the brass bell was hardly my last trick.

As the ghost circled, I matched him. This was made difficult by my limited range of vision and total lack of depth perception, but I was struggling to grab a handful of dried sage and cedar which should have protected the space we were in.

Ideally, I would like to have picked the place for this confrontation, but apparently the ghost of Holmes had run out of patience before we had found the perfect place to make our stand.

Britney made disturbing little sounds behind me. I had intended to ask her later if she felt this nonsense was real once we were safe again, but the despairing whimpers had answered that question already in a way that made me feel terrible for having even wanted to ask.

Holmes rushed in again from the middle of a water-stained wall and I dove to keep myself between him and Britney.

It worked, but the cold crept into my fingers and toes through the generous pathways left by the earlier frostbite. I felt my extremities stiffen and go numb before I slammed into the hardwood flooring. Not numb enough.

I rolled over, trying to keep Britney in my line of sight while I dug around my bag, waiting for Holmes to make another pass.

I didn't have to wait long, or even as long as I had hoped, before he shot out of another wall and tried to touch her.

Sometime I'd like to say that I gracefully did something, but if you've read this far, you'd never believe that so I won't waste time lying.

I heaved myself over and flung a damp, five-pound bag of salt at the ghost and was more than a little relieved when it burst and he faded into oblivion.

"Are you just going to randomly fling shit," Britney asked, "Or do you actually have some kind of plan here?"

"Little from column A," I admitted, rolling onto my back, "and a little from column B."

"Is he coming back?" she glanced around, covering all the things I should be looking at but couldn't anymore.

"I don't know," I admitted, "I hit him with a lot of salt and sometimes that does the trick. It's not like there are hard and fast rules here."

"I thought you knew what you were doing?" she seemed to be spiraling.

"Where did you get that idea?" I felt the best case scenario was to have her so upset with me that she couldn't spend more time in mortal terror. There are a lot of reasons that I'm single, but I can point to that one for sure if anyone is compiling a list, "I've done this before, of course, but every haunting is a unique and special snowflake."

"I don't think I've ever hated anyone more than I hate you," she said, stomping up another set of stairs.

"That a girl," I smiled, following after her.

Chapter 41

The thing about poking at the restless dead is there isn't a rulebook. And even if there was, there's no referee to yell at or centralized authoritative council or association or committee where someone could lodge a formal complaint when things don't go your way or even just seem vaguely unfair. Most of the time, if you've been screwed over enough to bitch about it, you've been dead for fifteen minutes and now you've got a whole list of other things to worry about.

What I was worried about were the hassles of the living who wander around in the liminal spaces where the dead feel more at home.

I had another bag of salt, my last, but if the previous one hadn't been a permanent fix then this one wouldn't be either.

I had a few bundles of herbs that I had mentally labeled "assorted" because not only am I not a botanist, I don't really know what any particular plant should be used for.

A long time ago I had some kind of ivy in my kitchen that I remembered to water just often enough to keep it alive. My cat, Angus, took to chewing on it regularly while I traveled and he would wander my apartment throwing up clumps of ivy and piles of cat fur and partially digested kibble everywhere. I knew that the behavior was ninety percent political. I was gone and he was pissed about it, and since he couldn't use a phone to bitch at me, he reverse-digestively redecorated while I was out of town. It taught me to meet others where they are, because not all of us can express ourselves through conventional means.

This went on for more years than I care to admit before I learned that this particular plant is, in fact, mildly poisonous to cats and should never be kept where they can chew on them.

I don't think he would have modified his behavior in any case. His digestive upset was probably an acceptable cost to him for the statement he made.

While I still hold my choices responsible for his death, it wasn't related to my house plant ignorance. He would pee on my suitcase before a trip or curl up for days on the slacks I had carelessly laid across a chair and forgotten about to leave an artful swirl of fur on them even without the poisonous plant to weaponize his digestive fluids. He was, ultimately, the most honest creature I've ever met and I miss him terribly.

At the end of the day, it's better to have someone communicate their profound disappointment with you than to have them tell you nice lies that make you feel better. Sure, it hurts a bit and, in this case, you use up a lot more paper towels than normal, but at least you know where you stand.

That's great most of the time, but down there in the moldy dark I knew where I stood was not great. I didn't have any clue where we were or, more importantly, where we were in relation to a murderous ghost who seemed intent on adding us both to his all-time record.

Most of everything in my bag was useless or close enough to be indistinguishable from useless.

Every third step or so I imagined I could hear the tiny clapper click against the little brass bell buried down in my bag.

It had been very effective spirit mitigation back in Austin, which I estimated at a million years earlier. As the struggles became more serious and the opponents more formidable, it had been less and less useful. I wondered if I still carried it for reasons more sentimental than practical.

But I didn't know what I would replace it with in the bag, as the list of things which can disrupt ghosts isn't particularly long. It's bells and salt and bundles of herbs a person should know more about before wandering into the dark places that smarter folk avoid.

I used to carry an array of technical gadgets as well. Digital voice recorders, EMF detectors, laser thermometers and "ghost boxes" to capture the words of the dead from the ether, but I realized that while they were still in my suitcase, I had stopped carrying all of them.

Once capturing evidence was no longer necessary, the toolbox just got a lot lighter. At some point, I had gone from needing to prove there was some spooky shit going on to just accepting that it was and then dealing with it.

I suppose it was a time saver, sure, but lugging around bags of salt was just plain heavy enough without a ton of batteries weighing me down as well.

A person can save a lot of time and effort just assuming the worst of every situation. And that's not limited to ghost hunting. When one assumes the default state is off-the-rails, they can be free to act without a bunch of nonsense consideration and logic getting in the way.

I decided if I survived the next handful of hours, I'd give serious thought to starting a self-help podcast.

As if on cue, a sinister giggle echoed out of the dark ahead of us.

Chapter 42

I had a plan. Or parts of a plan. Some kind of idea about maybe making a plan.

What I lacked in actual plan I made up for in priorities. By my count, four people were dead. They were people I didn't particularly care for, to be honest, but I was determined not to let this asshole continue to run up the score.

And, as much as I didn't want to, I liked Britney. I couldn't imagine a less perilous situation where that would ever be the case because she was, objectively, the worst. But getting her out of this alive was a goal that I had internalized, and it would be happening or my ghost would angrily wander under Chicago for eternity.

While he was still alive, Holmes had prided himself on what he could get away with. Staying ahead of the police was important enough to him that he built a whole Murder Castle in Chicago to keep his work secret.

The building had been a rat's nest of winding corridors and dead-end passages designed to disorient his victims. Walls were lined with asbestos not to slow the advance of fire but instead to muffle sounds.

Guest rooms were designed to be air-tight so that poison gas could be released into them. Whole chambers down here in the dark were filled with quicklime to dissolve the corpses and conceal the scent of his rot.

Contactors were hired and fired throughout construction so that he was the only person that knew everything about the Murder Castle until it was torn down.

The man had made murder an art and spent years using that to make the change in the world that he most wanted.

In the end, he was executed for twenty-seven murders and five of those victims were later found alive. He possibly killed over two hundred people, but the infamous Murder Castle was torn down by day laborers in an era before forensic science was a thing, so the remains of ninety percent of his victims could still probably be down here in the underground with us.

The police found bodies in the basement, but nowhere near all of them and they knew at the time that it wasn't.

He took his trade on the road as well, racking up kills in New York and, most famously, London during a brief window when there is no documentation of him being in the states as Jack the Ripper worked his way across Whitechapel.

Carrie Brown, allegedly a prostitute working near the East River, was strangled and disemboweled in her hotel room and each of the five victims in the Ripper slayings was also strangled before being mutilated with various organs removed.

In every case, the bodies were dissected by someone who, like Holmes, had medical training.

Holmes owned a cement company that is recorded as buying a lot of ingredients and never selling any product. Disposing of corpses in cement is more associated with the mob around prohibition but it is likely that Holmes was doing it half a century earlier.

In addition to owning properties all over the region, mostly gained through conning his marks and then murdering them, he made a lot of his fortune though insurance fraud. And I don't mean the common burn-down-your-own-failing-business insurance fraud everyone hears about. He would take out life insurance policies on people and then deliver their corpses to collect his payment.

In his own jailhouse memoir, he describes chopping up and disposing of a body with no more concern than if it were just some inanimate objects.

It is entirely possible that the first documented serial killer in both America and England are the same person, and he was still hunting for fresh prey under the streets of Chicago.

Chapter 43

A fresh giggle emerged from the darkness to skitter over us like a spider across the face of a corpse and we shuffled to a stop by silent agreement.

My flashlight could just light up the bottom riser on a staircase across the room but it may as well have been on the moon from the situation we were in.

I glanced to the right when a shadow hit me from the left, my blind spot was more prominent than I had gotten used to so I didn't see it coming and tumbled across the floor with no time to compensate for the fall. Splinters of wood dug into my arms and legs and rotted wool carpeting ground itself into my skin as I tumbled.

Britney screamed in the dark, sounding impossibly far away as I staggered back to my feet.

"Stay behind me," I advised, "He can't kill me."

But he could hurt me, and I was sure all three of us knew it. I was moving slower than I needed to and my field of view was limited, and the darkness wasn't helping anything.

It had been a very long and objectively terrible night. The pains were adding up and refusing to wear off like they did when I was younger. My shoulder still hurt from knocking into the side of the submarine and I should have walked that off hours earlier. Cold crept into my limbs through the paths that frostbite had worn into my nerves.

As I was knocked down from the left into a graceless roll again, I knew the worst of it was that I couldn't see anything to that side without craning my neck around like a drunken owl.

I tossed a bundle of sage into the dark and waved Britney towards the stairs. I had no hope that any herb would save us but sometimes it doesn't matter what you throw at someone's face – Even the dead can flinch.

My hand brushed across the big brown paper bag of table salt, but I tried to ignore it. It was becoming a reflex to toss one, but it had yet to pay off for me long-term since the sun went down.

It was another situation where I knew there was a clock on the action but had no visibility into what time was left on it.

"I have the devil in me," the entity spoke for the first time, "Always have, from when I was born."

He followed it with a wheezing giggle, stepping in front of me as if he wanted whatever his next move was to have an audience.

"Just look at me big guy," I taunted, as the ghost was maybe two inches shorter than my already generous five foot ten inches.

The yellowed grin beneath his prominent mustache told me that I had gotten his attention. If only I could figure out how to use insulting a person as a strategy for self-preservation.

Facing the Púca had been different from facing Holmes because the Púca tried to maneuver around me for some kind of positional advantage and Holmes just steadily walked forward, closing the distance by the shortest path between our two points.

He knew that this was a battle of attrition. He could hurt me, and I was already injured. He could wear me down and I was already exhausted.

But he was, so far at least, invulnerable and imbued with the implacable persistence of the psychotic. He could afford to take his time killing me, as he had been down here for over a hundred years already and, if anything, he had only gotten stronger over time, layering fresh souls over the ones he had stolen in life.

"They tore down your murder hotel, Holmes," I sneered, "as soon as they could get the permits after hanging you in Philly."

He giggled again, menace lining the sound, but for someone who wanted, needed to be remembered, having your works discarded has to sting a little, even if you're dead.

"I never needed it," he stalked closer, "I killed in places before the hotel, and I continue to kill after."

"You didn't kill me," I glanced over to see Britney mounting the stairs uphill, the surface still feeling impossibly far away.

We could stay ahead of him for a while, but not for however many stories of earth lay between us and fresh air.

"You'll die like the rest soon enough," his thready laugh was deeper, more serious than his chattering, mocking giggle, however predatory that had seemed.

"Oh," I tried to laugh back, unsuccessfully, "soon enough is how everyone dies, but you won't have anything to do with that."

He darted forward, going for my throat with both hands to choke the life out of me if he had to but only managed to grab the left arm I had flung up between us.

He just held on, squeezing until his face went red and my arm went mercifully numb. The warmth leeched out of me in a visible steam as I struggled to get away from him. I could feel the cold navigating the trenches the cold of the Idaho wilderness had marked me with, inexorably heading for my heart.

The smell of burning cotton caught my attention before that of burning flesh, but only just. The raven skull pendant had heated itself dangerously fighting off the soul-stealing influence of the ghost and was reaching its limit as a piece of jewelry.

I yanked my arm away from the ghost before batting at my chest to extinguish the smoldering flannel that was threatening to burst into full-fledged flame.

I took two uncertain steps up the stairs after Britney before the leather cord holding the raven against my sternum burned through and it clattered away into the dark room.

I was unprotected. I was unprotected and the ghost of America's first serial killer was still coming after me and would catch up with Britney a moment after it was done with me.

He had casually brushed against two people in front of me and hadn't bothered to watch either of them fall dead behind him. My death wouldn't delay him at all.

Desperately I dug around in my bag again, brushing against that stupid brass bell again and grasping for anything that might slow him down so we could escape and regroup.

"Why won't you just die?" Holmes asked, giggling again in a way that was finally becoming more annoying to me than terrifying.

I tossed one of the glass orbs filled with liquid at him and said, "Because it's your turn, asshole."

The glass shattered and the bottom of the room filled with mist, eating away at his form, legs first like hungry piranhas, as it clung to the stairs below us.

The ghost screamed once, but for an impossibly long time, as he gradually disappeared into the thickening fog beneath him.

Chapter 44

"What the shit was that, Lawrence?" Britney yelled as we found ourselves in another long hallway lined with moldy wallpaper.

"That was a ghost, Britney," I tried to speak calmly, as I felt her grip on reality slipping away.

"No, dickbag," she stopped, "The glass ball thing that ate him. What was that?"

"Oh," I caught up with her conversationally as I tried to physically drag her forward in the tunnel, "That was a Victorian fire extinguishing grenade."

"Wait," she hadn't started moving again, "What?"

"They were bottles filled with mostly saltwater but other chemicals that were supposed to be heavier than air, so they would cling to the fire and smother it. The automated ones were set in wax racks that would melt in case of fire, and the glass orbs would roll free."

"Salt water?"

"Just to keep them from freezing," I explained, "The other chemicals were also 'salts' in the way that smelling salts are salts, but the exact blend changed over time."

"And that ate him?"

"Ghosts don't like salt, so yes," I gestured for her to continue moving, "But if that specific glass ball was made after the turn of the century, you may want to get checked."

"Checked for what?"

"About eleven kinds of cancer," I pried a large piece of wood out of the way to expose another tunnel, "But that's a problem for later, Britney. We need to get outside."

"Do you often just toss Victorian fire extinguisher grenades at angry ghosts?"

"Oh, no," I shook my head, "I never got my hands on one before. I wanted to try it out as soon as I saw them downstairs."

"Your ghost hunts aren't fun, Lawrence," she grumbled, "No one would watch this bullshit."

I laughed, for the first time in quite a while. It was surprisingly liberating, as if I had been unconsciously holding my breath or something.

We broke through to an unused and unlit utility tunnel, at least judging by the old cloth-wrapped copper wiring that lined the walls.

Rodent droppings and worse things covered the floor, but the tunnel was straight and seemed to be going slightly uphill and vaguely north, both things that I appreciated.

My phone was dead, so I had no idea what time it was. I hoped my last flashlight would last until we made it outside, but while I assumed it was still dark above ground, I only really knew for sure that it was dark in the tunnels, because that doesn't change with the dawn.

I wanted to stop and rest, but as nice as that sounded I knew that would be giving my body a chance to inform me of all of its injuries, probably in excruciating detail.

My clothes, burned and filthy as they were, were soaked in blood and under them I was one giant bruise, so as much as it hurt to keep going, I knew if we stopped there was a possibility I wouldn't be able to get going again.

"So," I attempted to restart the conversation as much as to distract myself from how bad everything was going to hurt after I had a nap, "Any thoughts on what you'll do with your YouTube channel?"

She was silent for long enough for me to think I had crossed a line before saying, quietly, "We always joked about two of us hosting an 'In Memoriam' episode for whichever of us died first. It was funny at the time because we figured the survivors would broadcast it from the business center of two separate assisted living facilities."

"Okay," I nodded, "I can see that would be the perfect level of ridiculousness."

"Doug just turned thirty," she breathed, "and Lloyd was twenty-seven or twenty-eight, I think."

"They were too young," I agreed, "Things get dangerous quickly in your line of work."

"That's just it," she kept walking, "this was their line of work. I was a communications major. I was only doing this because I couldn't get hired as a morning weekend weather girl and work my way up to the Today Show."

"That's a very narrow career path," I stumbled along after her, trying to keep the flashlight beam useful for navigation without blinding either of us, "That's just you and Al Roker."

"I'm still not sure I believe in this paranormal crap, and it killed two of my friends."

"I wouldn't know how to function if I wasn't still skeptical," I confessed, "And I literally had a werewolf call me out on that bullshit once."

"Werewolves?" Britney scoffed, "You're full of shit, Lawrence."

"Oh, certainly," I admitted, "But never about werewolves. They hate that."

Chapter 45

When we finally emerged onto the sidewalk outside of an abandoned residential housing complex, we were met by Agents Smith and Jones again who, judging from their disheveled appearance, had spent significant time underground since we had last seen them.

"You certainly make a mess, Miller," Jones admonished me as he took in my own far worse appearance, "but the situation we were monitoring seems to have been resolved."

I didn't know if that was the Púca or the ghost and I didn't plan to complicate things by asking.

"What is it they say in tech? Move fast and break things?" Smith chuckled, "You don't normally apply that to yourself."

"I have a process," I defended, "I'll admit it isn't great, but it's mine."

"You've left a string of corpses underground," Jones said, "We will be here for weeks cleaning up the paperwork."

"Try the pizza," I offered, "It's wonderful."

"What about me?" Britney seemed to feel like she was being left out, and I was honestly a little bit jealous, "I was here too."

"If you come with us, we'd like to get your statement," Smith's tone was nicer than she had ever taken with me, "Then we will make sure you get back home."

I looked between Britney and the two agents, "You promise you won't disappear her to some CIA black site?"

"We aren't the CIA," Jones didn't answer the question.

"What does it matter what color a site is, Miller?" Smith added, but I hoped her joke meant that Britney was safe with them.

They had been fairly rude most of the time and very demanding, but I hadn't been carted off to Gitmo or audited by the IRS, so I took those as signs that maybe they were okay people who just happened to work for a part of the government that didn't exist. I've worked with weirder. Hell, I consider myself friends with weirder.

I dug around until I found a battered business card. The edge was stained with dried blood, but the text was more legible than it should have been. I handed it to Britney.

"I hope you don't ever need this, but if you do, don't hesitate to call or text," I didn't know whether to shake her hand or offer a hug, as social situations are kind of weird when you've just nearly died a few times with a near-total stranger. Also, I was covered in blood and worse things, and I've never been much of a hugger anyway. In the end, I softly punched her on the shoulder lamely and looked away.

Jones gestured at my face and my shoulder hanging out of place, more in front of me than to the side where it belonged. "You need medical attention," he started to dial a tiny flip phone before I stopped him.

"Yeah," I admitted, "I do, but I have something I need to finish before dawn if you guys could give me a ride."

Smith nodded and presumably went to get a car. Or tank or maybe a helicopter or something.

Jones looked me over again before leaning in to ask, "Are you okay, Miller?"

"I just need you to let me out a block away. I don't want any of the cool kids to see mom and dad dropping me off."

Chapter 46

I contacted my guy in the penthouse restaurant from a conveniently working phone in the predictably black SUV and requested that he unlock the elevator and kill the power on the top floor of the building before I got there.

Dragging only my own light source in there would simplify the movement of shadows as the guy said they saw from the corner of the eye regularly. More importantly, I didn't want to risk being caught on camera looking like I had just been violently dragged through a sewer – Which I guess I kind of had.

Nothing can quite make us look as bad as the truth sometimes.

The head chef, Mark, met me in the elevator lobby on the twenty-first floor.

"What the hell happened to you?" he looked me up and down, lingering on the blood-clotted improvised wrapping on my head for longer than was comfortable.

"I walked here," I explained, brushing past the real question, "Can I get in and poke at your ghost?"

"I mean," he hesitated. Perhaps there was a dress code that I was definitely violating, "Sure, man."

"Thanks," I shouldered past him for the doors to the dining area.

"We think he's an executive from the 20's who can't rest because of the policies of the company in this building now. . ." he started to explain.

"I don't give a shit," I didn't look back as I brushed into the room beyond. The rich wood paneling gleamed in the light of my sputtering LED lamp.

Bookshelves lined the walls with volumes old enough to be considered purely decorative around clusters of tables and chairs and there were pictures of aristocrats hunting foxes on at least two of the walls before I stopped bothering to look at them.

The ceiling fan overhead turned lazily and it took me a second to remember the power had been shut off for long enough for them to have stopped. I considered warm air rising to turn the blades, but they were angled the wrong way for that to be the culprit.

"I don't have a lot of time," I announced into the dark, "So if you're going to do something, do it already."

The temperature dropped and the cold air began to circle around the room, rustling the fake flowers on the tops of the tables and setting the coffee cups and saucers to rattling.

A corpulent figure materialized in front of me, his silhouette dark against the lights of the city behind him. Dawn would be lightening the sky soon.

Lecherous eyes glared at me from a rotting visage as the ghost leaned towards me, reaching forward with clawed hands. This guy had been a monster for the typing pool long before he had expired to haunt the old executive office space which was now a dining room.

The misery he had caused in life was too great to end with him, and now it was a problem for the rest of us.

He cackled menacingly for a moment before I hit him in the face with my sad, last, damp bag of table salt, knocking him back and ethereally through the windows behind him.

I saw his arms pinwheel uselessly as he fell and knew he would fade into a memory before troubling anyone on the sidewalk below.

The bag of salt burst against the glass and its contents spilled across the floor beneath it, making a mess I wouldn't be around to worry about.

I exited to the elevator lobby and chose to take the stairs down.

"He won't be back, Mark," I promised as I shouldered the door open and lumbered through, "and I won't either."

I plodded down the steps and went out the fire exit when I hit the ground floor. I was done with Chicago.

Chapter 47

Less than a day later, I had cleaned myself up as well as possible and changed into new clothes, including a Cubs knit hat that I pulled as low over my face as possible to cover the loose bandage I had taped over my still-seeping eye socket.

The trip to the 24-hour pharmacy had caused more of a stir than I had wanted and I just managed to use the self-checkout and escape back to the street before the ambulance arrived. I think I looked worse than I thought, and I thought I looked awful.

I stood in line at the ticket counter, hoping to swap my 7pm flight home to Houston for one at 5:45. It should have been easy, as neither flight looked to be full.

As the couple in front of me ambled off towards the bag check area, I assumed their place at the counter.

"I didn't call you," the woman didn't look up.

I stood there for a second before uncomfortably shuffling back to my place in line. After a bare moment, she looked at me and impatiently waved me back over.

"Hi," I felt like she was staring at me and figured that was something I'd have to get used to eventually, "I've been in your lovely city for a few days, and I had a hotdog and tried the pizza so now I'd like to go home. Can I be on the 5:45pm flight to Houston, Texas, please?"

"So, you think that's all Chicago is? Pizza and a hotdog?"

"No," I shook my head, "Of course not. Something something rich and vibrant history I'd just like to go home."

"Did you just say 'something something history' to me?"

"Also, rich and vibrant."

She took my boarding pass and printed another, scrawling something indecipherable in the corner.

"Enjoy your flight," she passed me the new slip of paper, and I wheeled my suitcase over to check it.

I was grateful until I learned that whatever she had written had flagged me for special screening at security.

Stopping at the closest men's room to my gate, I was just washing up when the lights flickered a few times and went out. Light seemed to not even spill in from the terminal outside.

When the lights flipped back on, there was no one else in what had been a bustling public restroom seconds earlier.

Almost no one else, anyway.

The Morrigan was two sinks to my left, casually checking her hair in the mirror.

My chest ached where her pendant had burned its way halfway through the thin skin over my sternum. I had filled the hole with antibacterial gel which stuck to my t-shirt and pulled weirdly when I moved, which I did more often than I had realized.

"Not a bad night, Lawrence," she cooed at me, meeting my eye through her reflection in the mirror.

"Yeah," I nodded at her, "Once I get a proper eye patch I may be able to pull off 'rakish'."

She looked at me for a long moment, cocking her head in a birdlike motion.

"No," she decided, "I don't see that happening."

"That's fine. I don't see fifty percent of what I used to," I went back to washing my hands.

"I can't have you looking like that," she pronounced, "Not if you're going to represent me."

"Okay," I smiled, "So you're firing me? Great. The pay is lousy and my boss is unreasonable."

She took a step forward and slapped me across the left side of my face, knocking me into the mirror. I slumped to the floor, hurt, for sure, but more with the plain panic softening my knees. I was glad I had just used the restroom or it might have been even more embarrassing.

The bandage had come off my eye and I instinctively blinked, cringing in anticipation of the hollow popping noise my flapping eyelid would produce.

It sounded like nothing.

I raised a hand and touched the left side of my face, having already developed the habit of being slow and careful about it. You only accidentally stick a finger into your own empty eye socket a few times before learning how not to do it.

Sometimes we develop skills we had no intention of learning ever, I guess. No one accidentally learns to play guitar or knit.

The socket wasn't empty.

I stood and looked in the mirror, from two eyes.

They didn't match, and the one on the left was still figuring out how to focus, but there was definitely an eye there again.

The old eye on the right was still a grey shade, some muddy space between blue and hazel but the left eye, the new one, was dark green, like leaves just preparing to change color and drop for the winter.

I hoped the similarity stopped at color. I also hoped it would get better at working with the right eye as it seemed to focus too far away or way too close. It was too blurry to tell when I tried to use it alone.

The lights flickered again, and the restroom was as crowded as it had been before The Morrigan had shown up.

And she was simply gone again.

I barely made it to the plane before the door was closed.

I love you, Chicago, but I've been to half a dozen haunted houses that are friendlier than O'Hare.

Chapter 48

A fresh pile of mail waited for me at home, the dingy loft in a converted downtown paint warehouse seemed to take on all the charm of a crypt without my cat Angus to keep it warm or at least lived-in while I was away.

I set the Cubs hat on the mantle next to the heavy ashtray, the Mardi Gras beads and the big pinecone from Idaho in front of the little figure of The Morrigan I had picked up at the witchy store. I didn't know why I was doing it, but it seemed important to me.

Sometimes our rituals are important even if we don't know why we do them, habit having replaced any specific reason or maybe just the pattern seeking part of our brains trying to survive in increasingly chaotic times.

It probably also explains addiction in some ways but I'm not pulling at that thread.

Instead, I poured myself a whiskey with a shaking hand before going to sort the mail.

Yeah, okay. I see it too.

I had a few bills to pay, or rather the notices of their automatic payments and an invitation to a college reunion that I promptly and aggressively ignored.

There was another shipment of the good food that Aengus liked that I would need to return. I couldn't bring myself to cancel the subscription.

When I had gone to the office to let the leasing agents know that Aengus was no longer living with me, one of them asked me what happened.

I remember saying, "He got a one bedroom in Midtown to be closer to family" and staring at her until she realized how dumb the question was.

The leasing office had later sent a condolences card that was still stuck to my fridge with a magnet shaped like a dinosaur so I guess no lasting damage was done.

There was a plastic package with some novelty t-shirt I had ordered late one night and promptly forgotten.

It had a duck carrying a knife and read "Let's do crimes", so I obviously had needed it.

The last box was larger even than the bulk order of cat food and had a return address in Idaho. It was heavy and cooler to the touch than the rest of the apartment.

I popped open the pocket knife I had stashed in my checked bag and started cutting through several layers of high-quality packing tape.

Inside the box was a bag made from thick plastic and what looked like someone's failed ceramics project.

Cutting through the zip-tie holding the bag closed and unfolding it, I could see a blob of clay with markings carved all over it.

My brain was evidently not firing on all cylinders and failed to supply me the answer before part of the blob looked up at me and meowed.

It was late, but an hour earlier in Idaho. Ben answered on the second ring.

"Why did you mail me a golem?" I skipped all the traditional greetings in favor of getting the information I most needed.

"I didn't mail you a golem," Ben sounded sincerely confused, which was a relief because the alternative was that our poking fun at each other had escalated to mailing monsters at each other and I didn't have any idea where to source a USPS shippable coffin, much less the vampire to stuff it with.

Certainly not at that time of night.

"Then why is there a small golem shaped like a housecat eating through the box of cat food in my kitchen?"

"Is this a riddle, Lawrence?" Ben laughed, "Maybe because he's hungry?"

"Did you mail me this box?"

"Yes," he seemed to start taking the problem seriously, "But I mailed you a box of mud we reclaimed from the river. A bunch of it had wedged up against a beaver dam and we figured you would know what to do with it. But it was just old golem mud and you know we would never inflict a cat on anyone we liked. We're werewolves, not monsters."

It hadn't been enough clay to form a full-sized human figure, but it was more than enough to be shaped into a decent-sized housecat.

The side of the cat food box gave out and kibble spilled onto the kitchen tiles. The creature glanced up at me before digging in, scattering food around but seeming to occasionally consume some it.

"Okay," I sighed, "Sorry to call you in a mild panic slash medium rage. I have to make another call. Let's catch up soon."

"Deal," Ben hesitated, "but we really do need to catch up."

"Is something going on?" I asked.

"Here? No, it's Idaho," Ben waffled again, "Lawrence, are you okay? I mean really."

I thought about it. No. No, I wasn't.

"Sure, man," I answered, "everything is fine."

It doesn't count as a lie when you do it to a werewolf. They can tell.

I hung up and wondered what clay cat litter would mean to a cat made out of similar stuff.

Chapter 49

I checked online for the hours for the South by Caffeine coffee shop in Austin for probably the twentieth time. For some reason, I just couldn't remember when Lydia worked no matter how often we spoke.

"I guess you survived Chicago!" she answered the phone.

"Yeah," I agreed, "That's the click-bait headline but the article is longer. What are you doing this weekend?"

I drove the roughly three hours to Austin on Friday night and booked a room at a hotel I was reasonably certain was not haunted.

I carried no ghost hunting equipment, no bags of salt or bundles of herbs. It was just me, a couple of changes of clothes in a small bag with my toothbrush and twenty pounds of wet clay leaving muddy paw prints on my leather seats.

The paw prints were of note only because the guy was perfectly able to move around without leaving tracks everywhere when that suited him – He just apparently hates cars. Or me. He could definitely hate two things at once, actually. He had demonstrated that ability several times in the few days he had spent in my poor muddy apartment.

I felt bad leaving him in the car but he seemed impervious to temperature extremes and, judging from the fact that he arrived at my place sealed in plastic for several days he didn't need to breathe if he wasn't planning to bitch at me about something.

"Stay here," I requested, dropping his favorite mud-coated catnip mouse on the seat next to him, "I won't be long."

I locked him in the car and went into Lydia's coffee shop for the first time ever.

It was small but meticulously clean. Art done in a number of different hands hung on the walls and the place seemed equally suited to tourists and people passing through for whatever festival was happening as to the healthy crowd of obviously local regulars, all sitting and talking quietly or lounging on the comfortable-looking if worn furniture.

The building wasn't new by any means but it was obviously well-loved and taken care of.

Ordering a black coffee and a cup of cream through the QR code on a back table was simple, so I settled in to wait.

As it was close to closing time, the service was possibly more rushed than normal, but it may have just been efficient. It takes next to no time to pour a cup of coffee, but mine arrived freshly brewed and late at night, which is always going to surprise me.

It was delivered by a tall, thin guy with purple, spiked hair and a lot of facial piercings. He didn't say anything and I honestly don't think I ever saw him again, because Lydia slid into the chair across from me and began looking pleased with herself.

"How can I help you, Lair?" she grinned.

"Dial down the smugness a bit?" I asked.

"No."

"I accept your terms," I conceded, "I'm in trouble with the Fae and as they are your client base, I was hoping you could get me ready to negotiate."

"That sounds like a fun Saturday," she rolled her eyes.

"The whole day?" my shoulders slumped in defeat, "Can't I just hire you as my fairy lawyer and have you send me a bill?"

"I mean," she shrugged, "Yeah, but whatever bounty they have on you, you'd have to match it first. It's an in-advance kind of thing. Not my rules."

"That's bad."

"No," she waved me off, "I can find out what that is in just a few hours."

"I already know what it is," I was gradually sinking back into the cushy velvet of the chair, hoping to disappear.

"Is it bad?"

"Yeah," I admitted, "The Púca assassin said it was a pound of silver and a pound of gold."

"Oh," she shook her head, "Then you're just fucked."

"I know!" I said too loudly, "That's a lot of money!"

"No, it's worse than that," she explained, "Gold and silver mean nothing to them. There are Welsh mining fairies that can pull ten times that out of the ground in an hour. By placing the price in something worthless to them, they are telling every other Fae court that their grudge isn't about payment at all. They want revenge."

"Okay," I was switching back to Plan A, "Then teach me how to make nice with them so they don't keep sending weird monsters to kill me."

"What happened with the Púca?"

"She melted," I shrugged, "It melted. Whatever. I gave them a mouthful of rusty nails and the problem went away.

Lydia pinched the bridge of her nose and rested her elbow on the table.

"So," she paused to assess, or maybe to piece together the situation from a new angle. "One of the Fae courts wants you dead to address a grievance, and so you used iron to murder their lawfully appointed delegate?"

"Everything can sound bad if you explain it, Lydia."

"This is serious, Lair!"

I finished my coffee before coming up with anything to say.

"I don't know the rules, Lydia," I was exasperated, "I can obviously make a mess of things even without meaning to. Help me navigate this weird, stupid world."

"I found out what 'themselves' means in Fairy circles. It means the speaker knows the court in question but has reason to not name them and yet also has cause to be respectful."

"So why would The Morrigan care about either of those things?" I asked.

"I can't answer for some Gaelic aspect of death, but the fact that she didn't should concern you."

"Ignoring that," I sighed, "Can you please help me get through this courtly bullshit? Please?"

"Answer a question for me first," she offered, "Why did you order a cup of cream and drink your coffee black while it sat here?"

"I have someone you need to meet," I stood up and grabbed the cup of cream, "He's out in the car."

Chapter 50

"He's ADORABLE, Lawrence," Lydia declared as the golem cat slid down the inside of the driver's side window, leaving a long, muddy streak.

"He's a golem, Lydia."

"Do you control him?!" she was practically bouncing as I unlocked the door to free the little clay monster.

"I've really been thinking of him as a cat," I shrugged, "So no. That's not what you do with cats."

"Oh, but he's not a cat at all, Lair! He's a mystical construct and he's yours!"

"Yeah, but I was hoping you'd take him," he was twining himself around her calves, not leaving so much as a smudge on her black jeans, "Or maybe someone in your coven?"

She looked at me.

"Or book club," I amended, "Or whatever.

"Don't be crazy," she reached down and stroked the thing, which seemed to be perfectly dry for her, "You shaped it into a cat, and it lives with you."

"It showed up like that!" I defended myself, "He was a lump of cat when I opened the box."

"Okay," she sat on the asphalt in the alley, reminding me of the first time we had met, "Ben said the wolves mailed you a box of golem clay, but when you opened it, it was a precious, adorable cat, right?"

The thing had curled up in her lap and was nodding off.

"Yeah, if you say so," I nodded, glancing at the muddy mess of my recently detailed car, "It probably sat in my apartment for a few days before I got home and opened it."

"And when you opened it," she asked, "what were you thinking about?"

"Shit," I looked down at a greasy rainbow in a puddle, "I was thinking of how I missed my cat, Aengus."

"You manifested a cat golem, bro," she rubbed its muddy cheek and managed to come away clean again.

"So, what now?" I asked, "How do I fix it?"

"His testicles are made of clay," she giggled, "so I doubt a conventional veterinarian will be much help."

"Not him," I clarified, "the situation."

"What's his name?" she asked.

"I don't think he has an actual name," I shrugged.

"What do you call him?"

"On the way up here, I called him 'Dirt Reynolds' and I thought that was pretty funny."

She looked at me flatly.

"Okay," I admitted, "He didn't seem to love it."

"Give him an actual name," she suggested, "and treat him with some agency. I swear, it's like you've never had a pet."

"Aengus didn't like being coddled," I explained, "He was always happiest when he could complain about how I was disappointing him."

"And you miss him," she smiled.

"I appreciated his honesty," I looked at the lump of clay sleeping in her lap, "and I do miss him."

"So, name this guy and start over," she suggested.

"Fine," I know when to accept defeat, "but you're responsible for any muddy kittens that fall off of him."

Chapter 51

Cnapog watched us from the hutch in Lydia's apartment which contained a vintage turntable, some very old Panasonic amplifier and radio and four shelves of vinyl records that I could not possibly find less interesting.

He seemed to be cleaning his paw, but his clay tongue wasn't having any visible effect on his clay limb, so I suspected the behavior was performative. Typical cat.

His name was Gaelic for "Little Lump" but he seemed to like it. And I gave myself points for accuracy because, being a cat, Cnapog would not be awarding me any points himself.

"You look like you're trying to lay an egg, Lair," Lydia admonished me.

I couldn't say how often I had tried to perfect the courtly bow where I vaguely crouch over the bent back leg and spread my arms, but I felt enough like a bird that the criticism still hurt.

"Let's take a break and go over courtly addresses again," she sighed.

As humiliated as I was, I was grateful for the break. We had ordered a pizza and Cnapog had eaten most of it.

The Fairy Courts had adopted the human system of feudalist hierarchy, and as I was unapologetically American, I was subconsciously resistant to caring about it. Or maybe it was just too complicated.

No, it was definitely my rugged individualistic patriotism.

"You're introduced to the Duchess of Flowers and she extends a hand. What do you do?"

"A pleasure to meet you, Your Grace," I kissed Lydia's knuckles lightly and, as specified, without saliva.

"Now assume I'm the Princess of Tuesdays and we have never met."

I thought for a second, looking for a trap.

"Your Royal Highness," I offered a small bow, mostly a head tilt and offered my own hand.

I kissed the same, somehow suddenly magically more royal knuckles again before Lydia grasped my hand and said, “And what is your opinion on this season’s World Series, Lair.”

“The Colorado Rockies are due, Ma’am.”

My sports prediction was less relevant than switching away from the more formal address. Which was good because the Colorado Rockies are absolutely not due. I’m not even sure they still play baseball, and you can ask any fan what they think because most of them would agree.

“Very nice,” she bent in a curtsy by reflex, “Now the same for the Marchioness of Texas.”

“Of Texas?” I was a bit incredulous.

“Now the same for the Marchioness of Texas, Lair.”

I gave a respectful nod, “Your Ladyship.”

No hand was offered and I’m not a big reacher.

“You’re about to say something,” Lydia stated. "I can see it on your face.”

“I’m not.”

“You’re a shitty liar, Lair,” she said, “Say it.”

“Dear Ladyship, where be the sauce of ranch most fair?” I laughed, “Mine hot wings lie barren and unslain by flavor.”

“If you aren’t going to take this seriously, why am I wasting a Saturday?”

I sat down and set a hand on Cnapog’s suddenly miraculously sticky head.

"It's fine, Lydia," I argued, "It's Irish monsters that have some beef with me."

"They have ultimate beef with you."

"And they live in Ireland," I reasoned, "I don't. I'll avoid Ireland and eventually, they will avoid me."

"Lair," she grabbed my shoulders, "These are beings that live forever if no one kills them and they hold you responsible for killing several of them, plus a Púca. They can literally hold a grudge against someone forever and most of them have nothing better to do!"

"They sound just like my favorite aunt," I brushed it aside as my phone rang across the room, "Let's call my ever going to Ireland Plan B and work on making Plan A last until I just die naturally of liver disease."

I answered the phone as it was a work call. There was a brief exchange of information, the details of which I would like to entrust to literally anyone else to explain.

I closed the call and looked at Lydia.

"Lair, I need to ask you something and I don't want it to be weird," she said.

"That's fine," I replied, and it was because I had no room to process it anyway.

"Are you okay?" she asked, "You show up here after a few months and you are covered in bruises and your eyes are different colors."

I felt tired. Tired of lying about it and just bone tired from having been dragged through a bunch of things I was unprepared for. But mostly I was just so very tired of pretending things were in control.

"No," I admitted, "I'm really not, Lydia. I'm not okay."

"How can I help?"

"I need us to work up some details for Plan B."

Lydia just stared at me.

"I leave for Dublin in a week."

Notes

This is a work of fiction. Any similarity to actual people, living or dead or undead is purely coincidental (and would actually be really kind of cool).

What isn't fictional is most of the locations in this book, including the haunted Hooter's. There are more than a few unkind words about Chicago pizza, but the fact that they are unkind doesn't make them untrue. Come at me, Chicago. It's delicious but that doesn't magically make it right.

I've been to the restaurants and venues described on visits to Chicago and if you're planning a trip for business, vacation, or to poke at dead things, you could do way worse than visiting the places where these particular ghost hunters chose to eat and, more importantly, drink.

The side plot ghost stories from around Chicago are part of the official local folklore and can be easily researched if you want to know more. Again, and weirdly, including the haunted Hooter's.

All of the accurate gun information in this book I got from my good friend Jim Taylor. Any gun mistakes were added by me. Let's all agree to pretend they were intentional or something.

If you have the chance to take in a ghost tour or enjoy a haunted pub crawl, please remember these are opportunities to embrace the local history, good and bad, and that is as true in Chicago as it is anywhere else.

Only ghost hunt in structurally sound places and with the invitation of the legal, *living* owner of the property. Make sure your tetanus shot is up to date, too. It could save you a lot of time later.

About the Author

Garrick Blake is an IT Security consultant and occasional ghost hunter. He lives as deep in the swamp as he feels comfortable in south Louisiana, his long-term goal of a statistically probably haunted hermitage finally completed.

The villagers speak of him in hushed tones and children cross in front of his house on the other side of the street. Except for Halloween, because he gives out full-sized candy bars.

Most people know him from his first book, *Echoes of Austin*, or from his small but vital role in season two of The Gilmore Girls, before his character was eaten by wild dogs.

He owns enough novelty t-shirts to delay laundry for months at a time and recently learned that a person can wear pants during a Zoom meeting. HR was very clear and unnecessarily shrill about that.

Fun fact: Garrick Blake loves writing about himself in the third person and doesn't feel weird about it at all.

His writing buddy is an incredibly long and extra reclusive gray cat with a name plucked from Midsummer Night's Dream, though he mostly answers to "you terrible animal, stop chewing on the power cables". *Howls of the Windy City* was also written in its entirety with the diligent-to-the-point-of-creepiness attention of a new foster kitten named Kate. And by "foster kitten" I mean she lives here forever now and is in charge of everything.

There is always at least one candle burning and all activity will stop for a good ghost story or a decent whiskey, as all activity should.

Thank you for reading the fourth Lawrence Miller Ghost Stories novel. The other three, *Echoes of Austin*, *Whispers in the Crescent City*, and *Murmurs of the River of No Return* are available wherever you normally find finer books, because they will totally sell you these books too, if you ask them politely.

Please leave a review on Amazon or Goodreads and, if you've read this far, you can go ahead and recommend these books to people you like in real life.

If you hated the books and finished them anyway just to complain about them later, I love your energy, and we should totally be friends in real life.

Check out garrickblake.com for infrequent updates for frequent progress and the occasional short story set in the world of Lawrence Miller.

For example, *Line Items,* set during the events of Murmurs of the River of No Return:

https://garrickblake.com/elementor-712/

Read on if you'd like a preview of the next Lawrence Miller Ghost Story:

Mourning Pipes of Ireland

Some years ago, a rumor circulated that there were fifty different words for snow in the Inuit language. There are a few things wrong with that story. First, it used the word "eskimo" and that's actually a slur, we just didn't all know that back in the 80's. We found it fascinating because there were different words for whether the snow was falling or on the ground, whether it was crunchy or slushy, old or fresh. We could see a point to fifty different words for something that was basically, at its heart, the same frozen precipitation with slightly different moods. And we knew that it was important to the native Alaskans or Greenlanders because the weather is actively trying to kill you there at all times so having the best and most descriptive information could save lives. Also, the number fifty may be a bit of a fudge as well because of how the language works. You've got your standard nouns, like "snow" but then new words are created from that root by appending descriptor words to it, so maybe there are fifty words now, but if someone needs to discuss old snow which is hard-packed and, say, purple, it would need a whole new word, flinging our total to fifty-one with just one weird weather event where the snow is purple.

Yellow snow already has its own word.

I say all of this not to be pedantic, though I do love being pedantic. Call that a bonus.

I talk about fifty different words for snow in Greenlandic because it is adorable when compared to the Irish language which has ninety-nine words for rain, covering every possible windshield wiper speed, the size of the drops, the amount that gathers and puddles in your driveway and the impact that it has on your life in context with how much of it gets on or near you. It is discussed as the weather is in all places but somehow more because a pub will amplify a weather report much more than any other communications factor devised by humankind.

The Irish language has exactly one word for "sun" and that is linguistically fine because they don't get to use it that often anyway. If anything, it is aspirational – something to look forward to or maybe just hope for. Nice if it happens but never really expected.

I had a local once tell me that Ireland would be a fantastic place if someone could just put a roof on it.

It should be noted that the Irish language also has thirty-two words for "field", to differentiate between soil quality, livestock population, historical interest and location, as well as how much it floods during those ninety-nine types of rain.

I was jolted awake when my plane hit the predictably wet Dublin runway and began to slow before a leisurely taxi to the terminal.

Why does English only have one word for the places people get on or off planes and why did we choose "terminal" for that? It sets a mood, for sure, but not a very good one. I'd like a happier word to use for the airport in, for example, some tropical vacation destination where a person doesn't care if the Wi-Fi works there because email is the last thing you plan to think about. Maybe one for an airport where the bar near the gate doesn't overcharge you for a drink or expect forty bucks to replace the stupid charging cable you left on your nightstand.

Actually, I'm pretty sure that second one doesn't exist, so maybe a single word for "made up airport" would cover it.

Immigration was a literal rubber stamp when I told them I was visiting for work and showed them my ticket for a flight back out in a week.

For a place with a well-documented leprechaun infestation, there is an impressive amount of tech work in Ireland. Most of the big Dot Coms have offices in Ireland and the tech-driven "Celtic Tiger" economy is the envy of the rest of the European Union.

I was in Ireland to work a project to bring the security standards of an Irish connectivity provider into the framework dictated by the other member states on the Euro.

Ireland has the fastest residential internet in the world, even if the free Wi-Fi at the local pub is still generally garbage if it exists at all.

But pubs aren't meant to be places where you stare at your phone and doomscroll for hours. They are social spaces out in what the terminally online refer to as "Meat Space", where you are meant to interact with other humans with little to no distinction on having any prior relationship with them.

I'd go to one immediately, I decided as I squeezed myself behind the steering wheel on the wrong side of the tiny rental car and tried to make muscle memory take over for shifting even though the stick was on the left side and all that stupid muscle memory from my old Volkswagen in high school was expecting it to be on the right.

I was too early to check into my hotel anyway, so I planned to work on drowning my troubles in alcohol and greasy food as I eased into the left lane and prepared to make my lack of sleep Dublin's problem.

I pulled onto the left side of the road like I meant to courtesy of the green shamrock-bedazzled wristband from the rental car company reminding me to "drive on the left" and accessed the GPS in the dashboard.

A cool thing about Ireland is that you can type "whiskey" into the search pane on the GPS and it will give you options. There are distillery tours and retailers and even some museum options, but I just typed in my hotel and then scrolled around until I found a pub. I know that doing that while driving is not safe, but finding a pub on the GPS in Dublin is easier than typing in "not near a pub" and watching the circle spin itself to death on your dashboard.

Ireland is a magical place. They export mostly booze and literature and rely quite a bit on tourism for their economy, and as such they have invested heavily in infrastructure, making the highway system one of the most modern and convenient in the world.

But that doesn't help in Dublin, where the buildings in the city center are close enough to only allow a small horse cart to travel in a single direction. Sure, there are no potholes, but street parking isn't really a thing, and the giant vertical public garages should all use a logo that looks like a monocle over a hand twirling a mustache.

I left my suitcase in the "boot" of my car in the closest garage to the hotel and wandered out to the street, angling towards the river to take in a drink or seven at the Brazen Head Pub. It is famously haunted but famously haunted is a far cry from dangerously haunted and they had a good selection of whiskey I can't easily get back home. And live music.

If I survived this trip and made it home without trying to wedge an eight-foot harp under the seat in front of me, I would consider this trip a success.

Actually, surviving the trip was still in play.

While I love to say, "it isn't important to establish blame right now, we just need to resolve the situation and get on with our lives", especially when things are clearly my fault, things were clearly my fault here.

There was a ten-thousand-year-old grudge in play before I blundered into the accountability area, and then I had flung a ghost werewolf into some fairy realm, getting a few of those pointy-earred jerks eaten in the process.

It wasn't my intent, and Lydia tells me that intent is what fuels all of the magic that we humans have. But it means nothing on the other side. Worse than useless, across the veil our intentions can be used against us, frequently weaponized against mortal humans with impunity.

Rip Van Winkle famously took a nap that lasted far longer than his intentions had set, and who among us hasn't overslept and missed a revolution one time or another?

But the American Revolution is almost "current events" in Ireland, where the land remembers things long past human reckoning.

The grievance I was supposed to address was some ten thousand years old, from when the first humans set foot upon the island.

When the first human settlers arrived, the Milesians, they had exactly one advantage. It was the Iron Age, and they knew how to work the metal into tools and weapons. The Fairies had their own fiefdoms established across the island, but iron could kill them, stopping their dancing forever in a way which they had never experienced.

Imagine being immortal and drinking honeyed mead and living your entire life as some eternal garden party and then having the unwashed masses show up and start slaughtering the help.

The Milesian chieftains met with the Fairy Lairds and came to an agreement –

The island of Ireland would be divided 50/50 between both parties and there was no need to look at the fine print.

Oh, but the fine print.

Lydia yells at me for blindly accepting the Terms and Conditions for just about everything, and the fine print is the reason.

You see, in the fine print, the 50/50 was that the humans would take the fifty percent of the land that touched the sky, and the fairies could have the fifty percent that didn't, exiling them forever into the underground of Ireland, the dark places where people shouldn't go.

Objectively, it was a dick move. But I wasn't sure making me pay for it would make anyone happy.

It certainly wouldn't make me happy.

I would have to rely on whiskey for that.

The Brazen Head is a very old pub on Bridge Street. Officially old, even. It was recently named as the fifth oldest pub in the world. The crowd was a decent mix of tourists and locals, and I found a small table next to a fireplace and took in the surroundings.

Wood that stains over time has a different patina than wood treated with a modern synthetic stain. Age is just something that wood doesn't lie about.

I ordered a whiskey and what would be the first of many orders of fish and chips I would have over the next week, at least if I survived long enough.

As I considered my whiskey and studied the map on my phone a little boy walked over to my table. I would guess he was around six years old. He stared at my face for a moment from under blond hair which had recently been disturbed by some warm knit hat his mother was probably looking after.

He wasn't the only child in the pub, but he was the only one near me. Eventually he made some decision and, without a word, picked up the second of the two chairs at my tiny table and carried it away, eventually setting it down in a corner across the room.

I suppose I didn't look like someone who was expecting company. He wasn't wrong in his assessment but that didn't make it hurt any less.

The room cooled in spite of the fire, and I glanced around at the thinning crowd before my eyes settled on my erstwhile chair and the figure sitting in it. He was tall and angular with dark hair and darker clothing and seemed to be scanning the crowd as well.

The pewter tankard in front of him was visually jarring as the only one I had seen in the pub, and he faded away before I could process it as out of time in the way the dead seem to be most of the time.

The ghost of revolutionary Robert Emmet is frequently seen at The Brazen Head, always watching the crowd for the enemies that eventually captured, tried and executed him a few blocks from where I was sitting.

Famously, his body was stolen before it could be interred unmarked in a potter's field and placed in the family crypt, only to go missing again later.

Having spent his life fighting and eventually dying for a free Irish Republic, his missing remains inspired the saying "Do not look for him. His grave is Ireland."

I was pretty sure mine would be too before the week was out.

www.ingramcontent.com/pod-product-compliance
Lightning Source LLC
LaVergne TN
LVHW040222110826
845146LV00004B/1254

9798902714651